I0785768

CROSS RADICAL

Stories

by

Alexandrine Ogundimu

Feral Dove
Seattle
2022

A SIDE

B SIDE

"What a horrible night to have a curse."

- Castlevania 2: Simon's Quest

BEN
AFFLECK

The fifth step of Alcoholics Anonymous is "[We] Admitted to God, to ourselves, and to another human being the exact nature of our wrongs," which to a Catholic sounds, on paper, a lot like confession, and as an ex-Catholic K had a lot of problems with that but she was so desperate at that point to stop the endlessly cascading decline of her prospects that she was willing to engage in any arcane, barbaric ritual offered to her so long as it would lead her towards some kind of solace.[1]

The actual form of the fifth step was predicated on the work produced in the previous step, "[We] Made a searching and fearless moral inventory of ourselves." This meant making a list of resentments and listing how they had wronged the listmaker as well as how the listmaker had wronged them, then a list of fears, then a list of sexual partners accompanied, again, by how the poor fucker doing the step had behaved inappropriately, and then the sum total was read to a trusted person, usually a sponsor, K's sponsor being a very cool nonbinary Satanist who was impossible to shock and had an incredibly open vibe despite also being kind of aloof, and K felt incredibly lucky that such an individual had taken the time to even consider helping out such a dowdy fuckup as K, she of the combination thrift store/H&M wardrobe, she of the floundering casual goth style [2] , she who tripped over her words and didn't know what she was doing.

____

[1] It was this or electroconvulsive therapy.

[2] Being that she wasn't out yet, her clothes were a kind of liminal collection which she hoped to one day replace with proper duds.

K saw the entire enterprise as tainted by the expectation she believe in the benevolence of a higher power, which had been a bit of a sticking point with the sponsor as they went through the first three steps[3] and struggled over what exactly her higher power was and how it operated. K believed that God was real in the same sense that superheroes were real, but also that God was a sort of idiot baby that had little to no interest in the comings and goings of humanity and would just as soon annihilate the species as choose to guide the life path of an individual member.

The sponsor assured her this would not be an issue, that all that was required was some kind of belief in some kind of higher power which would be anything, and that it was probably best for them to get on with it.[4]

They'd agreed to meet at North Star Diner up on Greenwood Ave, which was close to both of their places in North Seattle, because K wouldn't be able to do the step with her roommate home, a roommate who obviously did not approve of the whole god and prayer thing upon which AA was based, and was such a staunch atheist and alcohol enjoyer that it was slowly dawning upon K that she would have to leave him behind.[5]

---

[3] 1. We admitted we were powerless over alcohol—that our lives had become unmanageable. 2. Came to believe that a Power greater than ourselves could restore us to sanity. 3. Made a decision to turn our will and our lives over to the care of God as we understood Him.

[4] This would prove to be only somewhat true, as years of sobriety later K would have a crisis of faith and be forced to reckon with her conception of God, and would find hers lacking in the necessary qualities to remove the phenomenon of craving, forcing her to seek out alternative programs in a desperate attempt to stay away from the bottle.

[5] While some might have been reluctant to share such a personal thing as an entire inventory of their wrongs and the wrongs been done to them in public, K was almost proud of how badly she'd fucked up and took a perverse joy in the idea she would be overheard by some straightlaced hetero who would be scandalized upon hearing her history.

Her earliest resentment had obviously been her father, the authoritarian Nigerian, Mr. Internalized Racism, gay-hater, bad with money but quick with a guilt trip, who had both supported and tormented her through her time at the grad program in New York but who had not approved of her move back to Indiana nor her subsequen relocation to Seattle, the most hateful man she'd ever known, prone to explosive rages and binge drinking, a wife-beating cheater who would make K hold stress positions whenever he was in a bad mood or felt "insulted" by some perceived slight the child had visited upon his person, and overall he was just a really unpleasant guy.

The only slight that K had visited upon her father had been that one time, when she was a 13 year old boy, she'd had her first self-motivated drink[6] out of his liquor cabinet, a large (for a young teenager) amount of brandy which she gulped down expeditiously while watching the 2003 superhero film Daredevil starring Ben Affleck and Jennifer Garner, a movie she so enjoyed that she would watch it multiple times a month on the already outdated tube TV her parents had spent too much money on[7] even though some part of her sensed that it wasn't a very good film, however she was enamored with Ben Affleck, at first believing she wanted to be just like him but in reality wanting to fuck him, the androphilic impulses being thoroughly suppressed in this conservative mixed white-Catholic-Afrian household.

---

[6] This was not counting glasses of wine and beer given to her by her father.

[7] Indeed, everything the parents had they spent too much money on. It was just the way K's father was. He'd spent six figures on luxury automobiles, set them up in a subdivision on a five figure salary, and spent four figures a month on alcohol, overpriced meals, and frozen seafood. The family was deeply in debt.

The sponsor absorbed this without the slightest change in expression, the theft of alcohol being in fact such a common crime among the alcoholic that it almost went without mentioning[8] , and they recognized it as merely an inevitability along the path to addiction and so acknowledged the admission with a simple "Ok."

The film Daredevil remained a favorite up to the present day for K, though she now enjoyed it far more for its camp than out of any kind of genuine affection, the Evanescence soundtrack in particular being a delicious bit of un-self-aware melodrama, and so she continued to watch it all the time, not once a month but multiple times a year, when she would get good and wasted and want to watch a movie that wasn't her usual trinity of transgressive garbage boy movies[9] and so would put on Daredevil and stare with love at Affleck in his tight leather attire. It even became a hookup movie, that she would leave on in the background when she fucked girls[10] she met on OkCupid.

And one time in New York K got totally plastered and brought home a different kind of girl, a transgender girl, bottle blonde and non-passing but intensely pretty nonetheless, a girl who was in the same grad program she was in and who ID'd as a lesbian but neverthelss was totally cool with going back to K's place and doing a couple lines of coke, and K was super excited about this because she'd never been this close to a trans girl despite jacking off to them like all the time and saw this as being her shot, her own status still being obscured even to her and so seeming for all intents and purposes like an average straight guy.

---

[8] Yet it was of vital importance to mention it, since the idea behind steps four and five is that you're catching everything you've done wrong, so you can make amends later.

[9] American Psycho, Fight Club, and The Rules of Attraction.

[10] So in the closet was she that she only messed with guys at bars.

They did the coke and started watching the movie while talking and laughing, both of them at that point of being fucked up where everything is cool and good and nothing bad could possibly happen, and there came a pause in their raucous eviscerating of Daredevil[11] and K took the pause to mean something it wasn't and kissed the girl on the lips, which she allowed for exactly five seconds before pushing her away and whispering "No," out the side of her mouth, but K didn't stop even as it became clear the No was a firm and clear repudiation, but then she pulled back and apologized and the girl said it was fine and it seemed like they were going to go back to watching the movie but that was when K realized she didn't care if this girl wanted her or not, so she went back for another kiss and this time the girl pushed back super hard but K didn't stop and overpowered her and felt up her tits and reached down to see if she had a dick, which she did, and it was only a punch to the side of the head followed by one to her bad eye that made it clear she wasn't wanted, and the girl grabbed her things and wordlessly left, and it occurred to K later the next day, filled with shame and self-hatred that she had come that close to being a rapist, and they never spoke again.

The sponsor absorbed this story with little more than a twitch of the lips, not passing judgement but it made K wonder if she was actually listening or not and she felt herself growing self-conscious even as she plowed on through her wrongdoings.

One time she leaked nudes of some girl on 4chan and everyone laughed at her and called the girl fat and made image macros out of her face.

One time she made out with a guy in the bathroom then followed him around trying to get him to fuck her until one of his friends had to get in her face and be like Dude, stop.

---

[11]And there is so much to eviscerate in Daredevil, from the acting and writing to the action, with its rubbery CGI, to the aforementioned butt rock heavy soundtrack and its ridiculously outdated depiction of Hell's Kitchen as some kind of crime ridden den of iniquity like Gotham City or Chicago, and overall the only reason to watch it is again, because Affleck is a hottie in red leather.

One time she traced a finger along her best straight male friend's hipbone while he slept.

One time she jacked off in front of a girl who asked her to stop but she didn't stop and the girl just ignored her until she came.

The sponsor absorbed it all, didn't say nothing, just waited.

Her ex came to visit her at some point, and after a day of shopping in Herald Square and wandering around downtown they wound up getting drinks at the Greenwich Treehouse in the Village, and K was still very much in love with his ex but it seemed like all that was going to happen between them was sharing a bed, which she was more than okay with, and they put on Daredevil while they fell asleep, and that's why it was a problem when her ex got on top of her in the night while she was asleep, both of them reeking of alcohol, Daredevil still going on K's laptop, and started fucking her because her dick was hard and that seemed for all the world to be the go ahead on any guy, and she came to out of blackout getting ridden which should have been the greatest moment of her life but instead was nothing less than an instance of abject terror, and she said "No," but her ex wouldn't listen, and mercifully her dick went soft which should have been enough but instead what happened was the ex reached down and started fingerfucking her ass, vigorously, while sucking her dick and she said "No," again to which the ex responded by putting more fingers in, and K tried to get away or make her stop or something but she was so drunk she couldn't move properly, and by the time she feebly tried to pull the ex's hand out she was getting fisted and then she came, against her will, and the ex didn't stop but went on fisting her well past the point of it being pleasurable, to the point there was blood on the sheets[12] when they woke up the next day and got brunch at the Dim Sum place.

The sponsor gave a nod and it occurred to K that maybe what she was experiencing was sympathy, something she hadn't felt in a long time.

---

[12] Not that K was a stranger to getting fisted, but it had been a while.

When she lived in New York K would carry a telescoping baton in her messenger bag, which was illegal, but she did it in part because she knew she needed to be careful and in part because she was inspired by Ben Affleck in Daredevil who carries a baton disguised as a white cane for blind people because he's blind, and she never planned to use it but had it with her nonetheless.

And one time she was partying in Hell's Kitchen, and this time was special because she was dressed in what was technically drag[13] which she claimed was just a tribute to the old school days of the New Romantics since she was going to a New Wave night. And she and her friends went to the late night bar in the village afterwards, and they left to take the A back to the Upper West Side, and she elected to walk home in the boots that were cutting into her feet, and along the way she came across a white boy[14] who hollered at her and acted like he actually wanted to take her home but then realized that she was a guy and got really pissed off at that fact, and started getting belligerent and accusing her of tricking him, and he got closer, his body language turning just a hair towards violence, and instead of waiting to see what his intentions were K took the baton out of her purse and whipped him first in the ribs and then wherever she could make contact, and then she just started raining down blows upon him until she got lucky and cracked his skull and he fell over, bleeding, and she took her size 11 boot and stomped his face until he stopped twitching.

---

[13] Miniskirt, ripped leggings, knee-high boots with a three-inch heel, crop top, thrifted purse, glitter, eyeliner, eyeshadow, lipstick, black wig.

[14] In looking back she would take his designer tee and authentic watch as confirmation that it was the rich ones she had to look out for. A homeless guy wouldn't care, and a poor guy had so little to lose, though she would wonder if it was the inverse that was true for black guys, that it was ego and not money that drove them to certain actions, and once money supplanted ego in those guys they'd probably be okay with themselves.

Suddenly the sponsor bent over the table and took her hand. There was a look of absolute peace and understanding on their face, and they seemed for all the world to be in total harmony with everything they had heard, and they seemed to resonate in the real sense of the term, that is vibrate at the same frequency as K with all of these things they had done, this alone being enough to put K, who was crying and fearful and hating every minute of this, back into a state of equilibrium.

"You don't have to count that as a wrong if you don't want to," they said. "I've done the same."

And it was this, somehow, that gave K hope that everything would be alright, and that she would get through this, and that maybe it was okay to feel a sense of peace and tranquility about all the wrong that had been done to her, that it was okay to not worry too much about things, and a weight left her bosom as she sobbed herself dry at the table, the neighboring ones taking notice and shooting glances that she didn't care about, and suddenly it occurred to her that there was something magical about sharing a truth with another person, a person who understood, and if there was a god perhaps it was not so malevolent as to deliver her unto someone that didn't get it but to instead give her someone who understood what she was and what she had been through, and she snorted up snot bubbles that threatened to drop into her eggs, and she realized that her whole life would be divided by this moment, pre and post, and that she was intensely grateful for such a thing.

Alcohol and drugs had destroyed her memory and ruined her empathy, leaving K a husk that existed only to keep moving forward, a pitiful way to live but an all too common one she would have to spend some time unlearning and this was the first big milestone along that path to recovery.

What she didn't know then, couldn't fully comprehend, was the way that having a belief in something greater than herself would drive her towards peace[15] and cause her to work in ways that truly suited her instead of constantly working against her own interests. That everyone worshipped, whether they recognized it or not, but that she had the power to choose what to worship, and to let that choice drag her away from false idols and into beatific visions of prosperity.

There had been a time when she was happy, a rare moment where K's father was not onerous or controlling, but instead rather merry, in the summer of her 12th year, and the two of them had been driving with the windows down listening to "I Want to Get Next to You" by Rose Royce and the sun was setting on a beautiful summer day, not too warm, and they had both looked at each other with smiles on their faces and there was nothing for either of them to worry about, and in that moment K felt such a magnificent sense of peace and love such as she'd never felt before and only now since, holding the hand of the sponsor and crying, having finally at long last let go.

---

[15] This would not always hold true, but it would hold enough.

WOUND

When I entered the bathroom, it became a holy space. During adolescence despite there not being a lock on the door, my parents tacitly provided me with a single hour of time to myself.

Kids who are given time will make the best use of it they can. Watch the clock, spend the exact amount of allotted time on their preferred activity. Some masturbate, or style their hair, apply makeup. Others bathe until they are pink and raw.

I chose to attack my leg with a kit of tools I kept in my room, hidden in a shoebox under the bed. The nail file, the toothpick, the needle-nose pliers I had spirited away from my father's toolbox.

***

It began as grooming. I would pick the hairs out of my left thigh until it became smooth, feel the glide of my palm over unmarred skin. Shiver with a pleasurable charge at the sensation. The growth of my body hair, long and coarse, was by far the most upsetting discovery that puberty forced upon me. It was dark, thick, curly hair, not-white hair, immigrant, Nigerian hair. Hair that grew thick and lustrous from the scalp, demanded to be treated chemically, plied with heat and product, beat and trim into socially acceptable styles.

But it grew in bent, sharp forms out of the body. It scratched and curved, would not be ignored.

After a couple sessions of plucking the hairs with a tweezers, one by one, a great relief washed over me at the smoothness of my thighs. But then, days later, I found to my horror that they had returned, thicker than before. Worse, they were ingrown, unpleasant infected bumps under my brown skin. So to get at them, I had to dig into my skin with the blunt tweezers, tear out roots, bleed. The divine smoothness, then, would not last.

Ineffective. I graduated to a nail clippers.

In order to extract the hairs, I would have to break the skin. When the hair grew near the surface this was a clean process. But in time they grew deeper. Now I had to draw blood each time I removed a hair. The follicles would scab over, but the hair continued to grow. So I would breach the scab and dig, ever lower, until at last I could remove the offending strand. It occurred to me that I was going too deep, tearing too much. I would bleed so much, and the hair would be so short, that the tweezers would slip. And I would have to either pull for minutes at a time, or commit myself to ripping the meat out with the hair.

It hurt. I liked the hurt.

***

My father, in an ill-informed attempt to enforce heterosexuality, would show me music videos. Starting around when I was 14, we would sit together in silence and watch VH1. Mostly R&B, and a little hip-hop. Suggestive videos featuring scantily clad dancers and a firm narrative of male-female desire.

He was, like most Nigerians, staunchly conservative. He believed in corporal punishment. His only concessions to middle-class American expectations was to apply force infrequently, and to use an open hand in lieu of a switch.

My father, as he sipped moderate glasses of brandy, one after another, killing the bottle slowly with modest pours so my mother and I wouldn't notice, would postulate on the taxonomy of the faggot. Never the "homosexual," mind you. Faggot.

To him, it was a result of poor breeding and excess masculine libido while isolated from women. That's why priests fucked young boys, the pedophile being the cousin of the faggot. The faggot, and the lady faggot as well, represented perversion and rape, predators in gender-inappropriate clothing. They were the apotheosis of American decadence, and he was very proud that he wasn't raising one.

It is difficult to pin down exactly what about homosexuality my father disapproved of. On some level it was clear that he found the act of gay sex revolting, but it's unclear if he found the acts themselves or the actors more offensive. My father is a meticulous groomer who does not own a pair of blue jeans.

One day we saw a TLC video for a song called "Hand's Up." It prominently featured several male strippers. To me, there was little difference between them and the women twerking on that screen a moment ago. I filed those men, with no intention, under the same category as the other dancers. There was a similar, albeit distinct, attraction to them. I had never seen a man in an explicitly sexualized manner, never had the idea that men could be an object of lust. But now I did, and that knowledge could not be lost. And what was worse, is that I wanted to be the women on that screen, so that the men would want me.

My leg ached from where I had cut into it that afternoon.

Being that I was not a woman this attraction would breach the narrative of male-female desire my father was attempting to nurture. Fearing the application of his open palm, I wisely decided not to remark upon these desires, nor to act upon any similar ones until after I became an adult.

***

Soon my life revolved around removing the hair and skin from the leg, cleansing the leg with burning antiseptic, hiding the leg. Making excuses for the leg.

In time, the original purpose of the ritual was subsumed into the doing of the thing itself. I had a whole system, involving a nail file, rubbing alcohol, the clippers, and various other bits of metal. I didn't know why I would spend an hour or more removing the hairs from my leg, blood pooling on the surface to be staunched with alcohol and toilet paper. I only knew that I must do it. This is the nature of addiction: Whatever the substance was meant to alleviate is replaced, utterly, by the substance itself. Self-harm is strange among addictions, much like how gambling is strange, in that it is an action taken and not a substance consumed. However, the mechanism of addiction is much the same.

I would often question my own motives during this ritual. At first, I believe it was a simple wish to rid myself of the hairs on my leg. But then, why did I not shave?

***

When I was about 12, when the leg was still intact, my mother called me into the living room. She held an old polaroid camera.

"Take off your clothes," she said. "I want you to see what you look like."

I obeyed. I removed my polo shirt, because I was only allowed to wear collared shirts, as well as my khaki pants, because I was not allowed to wear jeans. The socks went too. I stood in the room, in nothing but underwear. At that time I wore white briefs bought in bulk from Walmart. The offending hairs had already begun to come through, stiff and uncomfortable upon my legs.

"Stand still," she said. The camera flashed, and the motor whined and spat out a single floppy picture.

It flashed again. The camera cheerfully produced another photo.

"Turn to the side."

Flash. Photo.

"Now your back."

Flash. Photo.

"Okay. You can put your clothes back on."

We waited together at the kitchen table for the photos to develop, white giving way to faint, washed out browns and yellows, the black of my hair coming in first. It was early fall, but the chill came in faster that year. The linoleum chill came through my socks.

"Okay," she said. The photos were arranged in front of me.

She did not have to tell me what to look for. The brownness of my skin and darkness of my lustrous, unkempt hair was considered a boon. It was the shape of my body that offended. I was, to be blunt, disgusting. My flesh lacked the tightness expected of adolescent boys, and was padded with fat. It fell in bulbous lumps where my pectoral muscles should have been, hung in rolls over the band of my underwear, bunched beneath the elastic of the leg holes. My proportions were strange, too much leg and not enough torso. And my posture was bad, hunched and crooked, accentuating the lumpiness of my frame.

"Do you see?" she asked.

"Yes," I said.

"You are fat. I do not know what to do about it. But you should lose some weight."

I saw something else that she did not. Upon viewing the shots, it was clear to me that I was not, and never had been, a boy at all.

That night, alone and fresh out of the shower, I examined the hairs upon my left thigh. The largest one stood out, an offending stalk in a meadow of fuzz. I found a tweezers in the cabinet, squeezed the hair by the root. Grasped, pulled.

***

As I dug ever deeper, the time for recovery grew longer. Until at last, my leg did not heal at all.

I tore off larger pieces of skin, cutting with the nail clippers then pulling them off with the tweezers. For the deepest hairs I would dig with the pliers.

The various smaller bumps, the open sores that used to be hair follicles, they began to converge. What was once a constellation became a galaxy, a vast swatch of broken skin, ever bleeding. I cleansed the area with soap and doused it with alcohol, the pain eliciting screams I loosed into hand towels gripped between my teeth.

At first I used large Band-Aids to cover it up, but they wouldn't stick. So I faked an ankle injury following an odious sporting event, then convinced my mother to purchase an elastic bandage. I fastened various pads out of gauze I stole from her medicine cabinet, before finally resorting to ripping up my old t-shirts to staunch the leaks.

Every day, I continued to remove the bandage and inspect the leg for new hairs. Wherever I found them, I attacked. The pain was now so constant that I did not notice the fresh hurt from each stab.

More and more of my allotted hour was taken up by this, forcing me to spend less time showering than I would have liked. My parents and friends remarked unfavorably upon the smell. I found it distinctly masculine.

***

He didn't like the way I ran, my father. It was clumsy, and almost like skipping, unmistakably feminine.

After a piss poor performance at soccer practice, he drove me to a different park. He pulled a ball out of the trunk.

"You run like a," and then he stopped short. The word caught in his throat, so implausible was it to him that I was anything but a strong, virile young man. He couldn't see me growing my hair, the lasers, the pain of breast buds, dresses, tights, sensible heels. He couldn't see me.

I dribbled the ball up and down the field, lungs burning, feet refusing to behave, the very image of unmasculine incompetence. Blood ran down my leg from the bandages, and a purple-edged blackening spread from under the edges, across what should have been healthy flesh. Fatigue set in as I ran back and forth, egged on by his bellowing commands, wanting just to rest.

At last I collapsed on the grass.

"Get up." He stood over me, monolithic.

But I couldn't. I was done, and it was over. The leg burned, in more ways than one. "Get up, you lazy bum."

I pulled myself to my knees. "Stop it. Please."

Quick as thought he buried the toe of his loafer in my gut. I bowled over with pain.
"Get up, you wimp. You sissy."

I dragged myself to my feet. He passed me the ball. As I moved to halfheartedly dribble, his
own leg shot out, taking out my shin, bending my ankle the wrong way.

"Stop crying. Walk it off. You don't want them to think you're a faggot, right? Then don't
act like one."

***

When I got home I bit down on a leather belt while I sat in the bathroom. Crying in hatred,
I brought the nail file down into the most festering part of the wound. Over, and over, and
over again.

 "What are you doing in there?" my mother called through the bathroom door.
I had allowed my hour to elapse. In a panic, I rewrapped my leg with an old bandage. Somehow this caused a new, searing pain I was not accustomed to, and I yelped.

"Just a minute," I responded through chewed leather..

The tools were lying on the counter, caked in blood. I ran the sink and began to scrub it off
as best I could, without any success.

"I'm coming in," she said. "You spend too much time in there."

"No." I threw the half-cleaned tools into the box and began pulling the leg of my sweatpants
over the sloppy bandage.

23

The door opened, and I made eye contact with my mother. Her face was a vision of fury. But then she looked at the open box on the counter, and my poorly wrapped leg, and her face began to take on another, worse character.

Without asking my consent, she moved forward and seized the bandage. I protested as loudly as I could, but she ignored me, pulling the wrap off with increasing speed. When she saw what was underneath, her mouth opened and let out a strangled noise I will never forget.

The wound was no longer red and angry. It had begun to take on other colors, blue and black and rotten yellow. Dark blood and pus alike leaked out and ran, gently, down to my knee, as lines of putrefaction channeled outwards. It was less a wound and more a crater, exposing layers of dead meat, down to something too pale and too hard. How it functioned, I did not know. I do not remember a smell, but it looked as if there was one.

I began to cry. She admonished me, asking questions. What was it? How had this happened? Why did I mutilate myself like this?

There was no way for me to explain. I had never heard of depression, or anxiety, or obsessive compulsive disorder, and certainly not gender dysphoria. I wasn't even aware of the term "self-harm." So I just repeated the only thing I could think of, over and over.

"Don't tell dad. Don't tell dad. Please, don't tell dad."

EVERYTHING WILL BE ALRIGHT IN THE END

(an unauthorized biography of Tiger Woods)

"You exercise your right to "freedom" and this is the result. All rhetoric to avoid conflict and protect each other from hurt. The untested truths spun by different interests continue to churn and accumulate in the sandbox of political correctness and value systems. Everyone withdraws into their own small gated community, afraid of a larger forum. They stay inside their little ponds, leaking whatever "truth" suits them into the growing cesspool of society at large. The different cardinal truths neither clash nor mesh. No one is invalidated, but nobody is right. Not even natural selection can take place here. The world is being engulfed in "truth.""

- Metal Gear Solid 2: Sons of Liberty

1

People keep telling me, I should write about junior golf. That I have a unique insight to use to my advantage.

I don't really know anything about junior golf. I just know that for almost ten years my life revolved around Tiger Woods.

2

By a trick of time and memory, never did I not know of Tiger Woods. When I was small, and my father gave me toy golf clubs before his breakthrough 1997 Masters win, I still knew there was a man named Tiger who was extraordinary, because he was a stellar golfer and the only black one.

3

My father came to this country in the 80s with nothing. Came from a family with plenty. This discrepancy makes him avaricious.

He craves things. Cars and houses mostly, but also fine clothing and jewelry. The highest good in life is to obtain material wealth. Through this he could obtain time, and luxury.

A great many moral considerations could be suspended in the pursuit of such a thing.

4

My father's tastes: pedestrian, bland, obvious, suburban, white, petit bourgeois, disgusting.

Middle shelf brandy and bad wine.
Previously frozen seafood fried into oblivion.
Subdivision address.
Middle range Mercedes-Benz sedans he can't afford.
Clothes from Men's Wearhouse.
Fish-bait-quality caviar to go with Korbel California Champagne.
Middlebrow films and international soccer and The Golf Channel.
Beethoven.

No books but technical manuals and dreck about management styles.
Yet he insists that he is an object of envy. The finest and most cultured of men. Only black skin holding him back from heights of greater mediocrity.

A buffoon.

5

Blood, and breeding. I am of a royal lineage, grandchild of a White Cap Chief, a kind of local functionary in Nigeria. Because of this he insisted I was "a cut above" my American peers. Smarter, stronger, brighter, a better class of human. My mother was of decent stock as well, her family being descended from Jean-Baptiste Drouet, Comte D'Erlon, one of Napoleon's lackeys and a colonizer.

In this way I learned about blood and breeding and rearing, and came to understand that some people are better than others by virtue of their birth, and I walked around with this delusion until I moved to New York at the age of twenty-fucking-six and saw what real wealth and blood and breeding were, and that it wasn't real, and that even if it was I wasn't a cut above so much as leftover cube steak gone rank with misuse.

6

My earliest complete and episodic memory. I am three or four years old. I go to the ice
rink for a lesson, fail miserably. I am pushed, crying, by the instructor back to my parents,
who bundle me up and took me to the car.
My father began to berate me.

It is a scene that would become ubiquitous in a few short months, endlessly and meaning-
lessly repeated, he stood me in front of him on the carpet of our apartment living room,
and screamed at me. He screamed because I was crying, because I did not work hard
enough at skating, because I could not take instruction, because I did not listen to him,
because I was an embarrassment to him.

Because I was a wimp, and a sissy, and I acted like a girl.

And he would continue this refrain for the rest of my life.

7

And so it became understood, from a young age, that I was inadequately masculine. I must become more masculine, and sooner rather than later. It was not a question, demand, or proposition, so much as it was an inalienable and unmovable fact of life that I would, in time, force myself into.

8

Tiger Woods. So small and young when he first appeared on television, an oddity not because he could hit a golf ball at so young an age but because he was black and could do so. Black man as golfer is to say black man as cryptid, black child as golfer is to say miracle. Come one and all to look at the freakshow.

It must have given him a great deal. Impetus. Momentum. Now his life had shape and meaning, now there was a final form to be pushed into.
Black man as golfer. Cryptid. Same as black man as happy.

Let's give me a name. K, because it isn't my name, but it will do. K was born dead, inexplicably given a boy's name and marked on the birth certificate with a bold letter M, scarlet letter only invisible and repeated on endless government documents. This was in spite of her penchant for skipping, her effeminate mannerisms, the high-pitched, lisp-tinged words she snarked at anyone who would give her attention. Somehow, they still marked K as M, just because she happened to have a deformed vagina that looked and functioned exactly like a healthy human penis.

10

Tiger Woods. The absolute legend, one of the greatest athletes in history, the man who broke the color barrier. Drug issues. Adulterer with a violent temper.
Just like my father.

Eldrick "Tiger" Woods. The child of a Vietnam vet named Earl and a Thai woman named Kultida. The father, older than the mother. Mixed race.
Something like me.

11

Little boys. Feral on top of that. The world theirs by virtue of the meat clumped up in their loins.

Misandry is rude and a bit gauche, but not unjustified. Men are dirty and rough by their very nature, testosterone filling the skin with oil and driving one to rage and above all a meaningless but insatiably violent desire to fuck. Pump a natal female full of it and you can see the results: hair sprouts, the eyes begin to glint and roam hungrily, and now you undeniably have a man in front of you. To choose this is to at least know what you are. Here is opportunity for mitigation. Here is purification.

But to be born that way and not to be worthy of hatred, you must either be gay, or a woman. At least, this is what I thought, male bodied and unaware of what being gay meant, but still instictually understanding in that childish way that some men fucked other men. Early childhood was spent in isolation, the precious being unworthy of the gaze of others. It was a theme that would arise time and again in my life.

12

What cruelty to be born male.

13

A synecdoche is a part of the whole that represents the whole, or vice versa. It can be used as a symbol for something to emphasize certain aspects of the whole, or it can be short-hand for a larger, more complex entity or abstract concept.

I abhor talk of "the body" as euphemism for the human being. It is synechdoche used for evil, a shrinking down and diminishing for the ostensible purpose of creating emphasis. The body of a human being is the sum total of a human being, and not a portion of it. The soul is a function of the body, created by an organ known as a brain which generates consciousness for the evolutionary purpose of more effectively surviving the treachery of the natural world.

To talk of the black or queer or female "body" is to remove the humanity in an effort to create sympathy. We are not bodies. We are human beings, with all the complexity that implies. Inside each of our skulls are memories, thoughts, innovations and connections in flux, combining and recombining into infinite novel forms.
We arc universes.

For most of my life Tiger Woods was synechdoche for my entire being.

15

The doctors called K a miracle. The mother had endometriosis and given that and her advanced age had trouble conceiving. There was no labor, just an overlong pregnancy full of tests and gently husbanding her to term. They had to shoot her full of hormones, her face growing hair as a result that never faded away.

Maybe that's why her daughter was born with a penis.

What great misfortune to be born malformed.

17

My mother did not hurt me in any kind of meaningful way. She did not raise me, she did not hover over me, she did not make me what I am, she was not an all consuming force nor a lodestone by which I set my course. She did not make me what I am.

The madness that consumed me is unique to black men. It is the result of enormous pressure placed upon him, the contradiction of being treated as a draft animal while having the constellation of a human soul. They become hard, and worldly, whip smart, avaricious, combative, because that's what's needed for a certain kind of soft young black man who feels deeply and is treated as farm equipment.

Black women carry the contradiction differently, and anyway my mother was white so what does she know?

She was nothing but loving and caring and beautiful and wonderful and it is for those reasons I will not disrespect her by writing about her as if she is meat to be pulled apart, the way my father is, and Tiger Woods is, and I am.

46

K's father who could only see that letter M. Her wholeness never entertained in any meaningful way, and instead it was smushed aside in favor of the all-consuming reality of that letter M, repeated endlessly across admission documents and release forms as the child was shuffled from one ill-fitting gifted program to another.

K's father was a real person, who was a prince, forced out of his country into the United States. That made K not only a prince, but the scion of a new branch house of Ogundimu.

Princes don't wear dresses. They don't put on makeup and high heels, and they don't fuck themselves with rubber cocks. They don't marry lesbians with partially shaven heads, or make out with boys in darkened restrooms. Princes have spines of steel and big meaty dicks and heaving balls full of children ready to be inflicted upon the world at large.

19

I often think of hands. The length of fingers and widths of palms. Of the thickness of nails. Hairs.

When I was young, I was obsessed with the hands and feet of everyone, but mostly women. I understood power in acrylics. To wear heels was to announce that one has come with strength. In my pre-adolescent sexuality, it was hands and feet that brought me the most interest.

I would judge the size of my hands against the children in my class, especially the girls, and I would find them huge. What an embarrassment.
When I discovered the tits of women and the asses of girls and boys I was fascinated, because I am an animal.

The reason I am not attracted to men despite desiring their legs and butts and chests and adonis belts and penises and testosterone-engorged clitorises is because of the hands. They are never quite delicate enough. Never domestic enough, or loving enough, or scornful, or twisted with work rather than thickened.

Lesbian erotica focuses on the hands of women. I find this incredibly appealing. I think I would have understood this when I was younger more readily than desiring someone's thinness.

So for K, obsessed as she is with hands, it wasn't until she applied her first set of pointed acrylic fingers to the warmth between her beloved partner's legs that she truly felt like a woman.

20

Tiger Woods became synechdoche for the entire black American experience. He rose to absolute dominance in the whitest sport in the world. It was not enough for him to be an excellent player. For Tiger Woods, nothing less than the literal peak of the entire world of athletics would do. Utter domination the likes of which had never been seen before, records smashed at an astonishing rate, major tournaments humiliated by the scores he put up, rivals dispatched with no fanfare and less dignity.

Tiger had something to prove. Not just for himself, but for all of us, for all the black children of the world. To prove that you can invade the space of white people and claim it as your own. Reverse-colonization.

And he completed this task so thoroughly in his golden years, in the time when his name was synonymous with the game, as in literally, as in the one golf video game anyone bought had his name on it, that a strange thing happened. What had been exceptional became mundane. Something there to be watched with awe now became something attainable.

21

K's father believed, as so many black men believe, that sports was the way out. Through sport, his child could ascend past middle-class mediocrity and into the stratosphere of wealth and fame. Nothing less than the best for my child, he said.

He held her in his arms when she was a baby, and promised her this: That whatever K needed, she would get it from him. All the things he hadn't had, and that included all the smiles and love he had wanted and never received. And of course fame too, the highest form of love. Love from strangers. Infinite. Refundable.

The promise is weaponized against her, to show how she is ungrateful. Can she not see that her father wants only to make her the finest M he can muster, so that she may re-vanchize the fallen house of Ogundimu?

KO. Knockout.

It's a shield too, the promise I mean. It defends her from the things her father really wants to do.

My mother is white. This is incidental and irrelevant.

23

I don't know how to document my child and teenage years without acknowledging that my father was severely mentally ill. I think I am afraid that if I don't I will fall into the same sickness, and be forever lost.

24

My whole youth I was assured that I was exceptionally skilled at golf. That my swing was so perfect, my natural talent so uncanny, that I must surely be destined for nothing less than the absolute heights of the game, entering the halls of the greats. I was to stand astride the earth, a colossus of athletic ability, the pinnacle athlete of my generation. And with this would surely come much wealth and fame and glamour.

The alternative was obscurity, failure, toil, and the endless, indescribable suffering my father endured as a man employed full time at a white collar job.

At some point early in my childhood, my father embarked upon a project. It was difficult to see the shape of it all at once, but it had to do with athletics. It was imperative that I learn to play a sport.

After failing at tennis, hockey, basketball, and soccer, he settled on golf. We chose this because I didn't have to chase the ball.

At some point, the project morphed from simply raising an athletic child, to molding me in the image of one Tiger Woods, the finest athlete of his generation. I was to be exactly as he was, his equal in skill, to bring glory to my family, to operate with my father as part of a two-man team as Tiger Woods and his father Earl did.

26

Work, regular work, was described to me in terms of Gehenna. It was a cauldron wherein the living dead suffered untold punishment, ground to powder within a great and terrible machine. It was the absolute worst fate one could reach, one that most fell to, but that I would be mercifully saved from by my burgeoning career as the next golfing phenom.

The wager was simple. I would give up my childhood, those precious golden years, in daily toil. Every day, six to eight to twelve hours at a time, I would practice. I would strike balls in freezing cold weather until my hands bled. And in return, I would live a life of absolute bliss and luxury, not forced to do that terrible work.

So what if I wouldn't experience childhood? I was to be a god.

To ensure the success of his project, my father insisted I be homeschooled. An only child kept away from the world, insulated from racism and judgement, uncorrupted by popular media and trends, sheltered from drugs and sex and violence. A machine that played golf, a finely tuned bit of clockwork too precious to be allowed in the outside world where dust and grime could muddy the works.

Homeschooling insulated me from everything. Even from exercising the limits of my strangeness. 24 hours a day, I was linked to one parent or another, never given the opportunity to learn any of those countless ineffable skills kids learn. Yes, I did not have to suffer the cruelty of other children. But neither did I glean a single tool I needed to be an adult. I had no choice but to put myself together and of course I failed miserably.

29

My typical day was like this:

Get up.

Attempt, and fail to complete a full day of lessons.

Put on khakis and polo shirt.

Ride in the car to the driving range.

Hit golf balls for the next five to eight hours.

Fail to meet expectations.

Be endlessly berated by my father over how I failed to listen to his instruction.

Absorb instruction as to how I was ungrateful.

Didn't I know that many kids would kill for this opportunity?

Consume some sort of overpriced meal.

Listen to a list of my flaws as my father became increasingly drunk.

Go to bed.

Know that something wasn't quite right, but be unable to name the flaw.

In hindsight, I'm glad I quit playing of my own volition. I would have had to share my father's delusion to keep up the charade.

What an inheritance that would be.

Was it strange to grow up as I did, or is it possible that everyone else came up strange? The answers are clear to me now, having had the benefit of adulthood to look around myself and to realize that a certain mediocrity is not only inevitable, but desirable. Better to not crave such unreachable pinnacles. Keep your eyes on your own work, for even if that pinnacle is within your grasp there can be no reaching it except by first being mediocre. One must pass through such a state, even the preternaturally gifted, before being delivered into any kind of exceptionalism. And even then, the mediocrities of the world stand head and shoulders above most of us, seven plus billion humans, almost all of us suffering under the capitalist means of production.

I grew up lacking in this single crucial piece of knowledge, this love of the mediocrities, and that is why I have suffered.

Two little girls named Dori and Tara were the first friends I ever made. Like so many friendships of those early years of life, they became my friends through sheer dint of proximity. They happened to live in an apartment building in the same complex as mine, one building over to be exact, and we met I believe on a playground not far away. Nothing really eventful happened between us. That they were girls and I a boy was insignificant.

One time when we were playing (something about the tails of squirrels) I think I touched the younger one's vagina and we both got really quiet, and then it never came up again.

33

To me, the only difference between boys and girls was that one had a pee-pee on the outside and the other on the inside. That, and the girl's toy section was a loud riot of pink that made me nauseous with its stink.

Individual girls toys did not upset me. Only the plurality. To this day I abhor the color pink.

<h1 style="text-align:center">34</h1>

I bet that Tiger Woods doesn't experience existential crises. I bet he's never unsure of himself or depressed or desperately looking for a way out. I bet he can control his drug problem without the aid of a spiritual program of recovery. I bet his father was nothing but good to him. I bet he never wakes up from night terrors after stabbing his father to death. I bet he doesn't have PTSD or depression or gender dysphoria. I bet he's secure in his sexuality, and I bet he has good relationships with his hundreds of former partners. I bet he smells nice. I bet he doesn't spend lots of time worrying about his chemical intake or the side effects of all the drugs he's on. I bet he and his father still speak all the time even though his father is dead and I bet he's happy.

35

The first time my partner, whom I hope to marry, fucked me, it felt like I finally lost my virginity.

Technically we both knew what we were doing, because I'd fucked women before, and they'd been married to a man. But there was an agreement beforehand that this would be different.

Where I kissed them. How much time I spent rubbing their chest, taking each nipple between my thumb and forefinger. And how they caressed the buds on my own chest, and how I didn't recognize any of these smells, and how the wetness that came from me suddenly resembled what I was so fond of between all those other girls' legs.

To this day I feel a great sadness that the first time around, it was nothing like this.

I have never had gay sex. But I have had trans sex, same gender sex, as a man and as a
woman. Through a trick of timing I only know how to use one set of genitals.
This is not the raucous, slutty, deeply satisfying kind of read.
This is sad and slight and full of gaps.

Trans sex is not straight sex, at least not for me.

And I will admit that part of me misses those underwear, those boots, the coarse hair, the
dank sweat, flat chest, facial hair bristling against each other.

I always wonder, if I had gone that way, if I would have bothered transitioning. And then I
look at my own skin, and my own hair, and my own clothes, and I know that I was always
meant to be one thing but lived like another, and that like any fantasy, it was fun at times.

My father preens like a fag, as my mother would put it. He is meticulous in his grooming, applying lotions, shaving with an almost superhuman patience, tweezing delicately, trimming nails then applying clear polish, massaging his limbs, brushing hair then applying, for baffling reasons, white people hair products.

Sit ups, push ups, picking clothes, never jeans, always a collared shirt, preferably not sneakers, sunglasses, watch. An utter preoccupation with the corporeal. Spiritual enlightenment in a tube of pricey aftershave. Elevate your consciousness by avoiding t-shirts.

You are black and will be judged at a higher standard. You are a man and must represent your family. You are, what exactly? The sum total of your suburban petit bourgeois accoutrements.

In acts of rebellion I refused to apply lotion. I refused to slick my hair with gels, or to do more than wash myself and brush my teeth. I didn't indulge any feminine predilection because wearing cosmetics doesn't make you a woman.

Now it is just another thing I reclaim from my father.

My mother has called me the N word. This is incidental and irrelevant.

40

To become Tiger Woods took a military level of precision and discipline. There are stories of the countless hours his father, Earl, drilled him through shot after shot, driving ball after ball on the munis and driving ranges of Southern California.

This is a necessary process to become anything like skilled when playing golf. You must be able to, under pressure, place a ball where you want without conscious thought. Execute like a machine. Drop that sucker below the pin. Walk your drive out there about 275 and through the dogleg, set yourself up for that short iron approach.

Ball striking is achieved through repetition. Endless drills, again and again, every club, until you know exactly how far the ball will go, how high, with how much curvature, every single time. You must reach virtuosity in this. You must know, not think, know where that ball is going to wind up every time.

It will not be perfect every time. There will be errant shots, mishit balls, misjudged wind. The goal then is to reduce the number of times this happens to as low a number as humanly possible. And the more times you can reduce this number, the less strokes it takes to put the ball in the hole.

It's nearly impossible to achieve.

But even the worst player you can find skulking around a regional mini tour, they are a better ball striker than nearly any other human on Earth. A game played by millions, and they are one of the few hundreds who have reduced that number to the point where they can eat Subway every night and drive around the United States in a secondhand motor home.

On his first day of kindergarten Tiger Woods was tied to a tree by a bunch of eleven year olds and they spray painted the n word on him and pelted him with stones, because Tiger Woods is a black man, and that is what is done to black men in this country.

I am light skinned and have been saved the cruelty of much racism because the children could not figure out which racial epithet to throw at me. So instead they just called me a wimp, and a sissy, and a girl, because it was easier and kids are cruel and anyway at least all those things are true.

43

To enumerate the successes of the young Tiger Woods's amateur career is, I feel, unnecessary, except to state that they are real. A brilliant junior golfer is not something that enters the public consciousness, save for the most dedicated of the game's fanatics. I only know of them because I had two biographies of Tiger Woods, one authorized and one not, that gave me the impossible standard I was to live up to.

I pored over those books, because I was one of the game's most dedicated fanatics, and because I was looking for the pattern, the explanation, that would turn me into this man that I had never met but so desperately wanted to be.

Contrary to what some might believe, I have no animosity towards cis women. They have been women longer than I have, and therefore have a great deal to teach me.

Tiger Woods was the standard by which I was judged. Every action, my choice of clothing, my swing, my putting, my short game, my mental game. I was to be Tiger-like in all things. Tiger Woods became my god. Every night, as I slept, I was to contemplate the mechanics of his swing and how best to apply them to myself. By day I pored over his biographies and his own instructional book, How I Play Golf, modeling each action after his own. Together my father and I wound and rewound VHS tape of his swing, breaking it down frame by frame. His accomplishments became my goals. I wanted to win more tournaments, make more money, shoot lower, drive farther. The greatest athlete of my time, and possibly ever, became the model for my own person. To not reach these heights was failure.

As I grew older I passed the age at which Tiger Woods met his milestones. I did not play in any American Junior Golf Association tournaments, much less win them. I could not place in the city junior tournament's top bracket, much less win the US Junior Amateur Championship. I couldn't even win a local event. And with each loss, the revelation of my limited skill became more and more alive.

I am bad at golf. That's just a fact. I shoot low 80s on a good day, and have failed to break 100 in tournament play. I lack the physical endurance, mental focus, intuition of angles and distances, depth perception, dexterity, flexibility, strength, and technical ability to play at anything higher than a weekend warrior standard.

So basically as far as my father is concerned, he for whom life is nothing but excellence in all things and golf most paramount, I'm dead.

My mother is incidental and irrelevant.

49

Tiger Woods has a mother named Kutilda. She is a Thai woman whom his father Earl met while fighting the Vietnam War.

No one ever calls Tiger Woods a chink, because he is a black man in America, and his mother is incidental, and irrelevant.

50

K has her father's hate, and for the same people he does. For her father, as he had it for his father.

For the whites. For America. K will not apologize for the hate, because it was earned with such determination and vigor.

51

There is only one thing Tiger Woods and I have in common.
I have a drinking problem.

The particulars do not matter. I drank too much, and too fast, and damaged my relationships and abilities until there was little of me remaining. I drove drunk. Then I found
drugs and occasionally used those the same as I used alcohol, although my drug of choice
was always liquor. I have driven drunk more times than anyone could count.

I don't know if Tiger Woods has a drinking or drug problem. All I know is he's had drugs
in his system while behind the wheel of a car, and that's usually a sign that something is
wrong.

What self-hatred I do experience comes from inadequacy. I failed to become a simulacrum of Tiger Woods, and therefore everything I do is tainted by the stink of failure. I am a mistake, that which should not be, a failed experiment and something to be pitied.

53

I quit because I didn't break 100 in a local tournament. It was hot, I was tired, and it was clear to me that if I wasn't shooting low 70s consistently by the time I was 15, then I was not destined for the lifestyle I'd been crafted for.

So I told my mother, who had me call my father at work and tell him. He said almost nothing, just a quiet okay.
Nothing was ever the same.

54

I lost a lot when I quit. Impetus. Meaning. Identity, because if I wasn't an up-and-coming golf prodigy than what was I? Just another teenager, pimply, weird shaped, smelly, rapidly gaining weight. No reason for me to be, just an unavoidable fact that could not be erased. What I lost the most was my father's attention. I went from being doted upon, his pride and joy, his pet project, to nothing. He lost interest in me almost immediately, offered nothing whatsoever to fill the gap. Whatever happened to me was no longer his responsibility.

I had fallen into Gehenna.

Besides golf, my father's favorite educational topic was mathematics. He was a ruthless instructor, drilling me endlessly, responding with anger whenever I failed to understand something. He would set me a task that I would find myself unable to finish, no doubt due to latent disabilities plus his inefficient teaching methods.

It seemed he wanted most of all to appear expert in all things, telling me how unfavorably I compared to his own skills at the same age. The affect was more important than the effect.

I was, and still am, a terrible mathematics student.

The homeschooling was a categorical failure. Neither of my parents possessed the experience or knowledge necessary to shepherd a child through anything resembling a robust education. Instead I received piecemeal instruction, unschooling, as my mother flitted from one curriculum to another, emphasized history one week and composition the next. She was gentle enough that I gleaned a working knowledge of several topics.

When I lost my identity, I gained it back the only way I knew how. I watched my father, quietly. I absorbed his ways, his means, ascribed meaning, broke down method. If I could not be like unto my god, Tiger Woods, then I would emulate his high priest, my father. The sum total was that I became a wrathful, spiteful, bitter young man, and I continued to be one until I stopped being a man and started being a woman.

58

Part of becoming a woman was getting rid of all those ways of being I had adopted in desperation. Naked force and smug manipulation, a supercilious attitude of inherent grandiosity, these things must be stripped away.

It is not that women are not capable of such things. It is that I did not want to be the kind of woman who was capable of such things. I wanted to be a better woman than I had ever been a man, and since I had always been a woman, it was almost easy to let all that shit go.

59

I started drinking in earnest at 19 and continued to do so until I reached the age of 25, when I took a brief hiatus.

The reasons for my drinking were these: medicinal, and spiritual. I sought connection and enlightenment through chemical means, because my life was entirely devoid of these things. I was not aware that I was a woman, but I was aware of my dysphoria. Not only my body, with its distinctly masculine fat distribution. But I had also learned that to function as a man required a kind of bravado, an aura of competence that may be unearned but must be present nonetheless.

Through alcohol, consuming it in massive quantities, I could prove that I was tough, that I was a real no-shit guy, that I didn't care all that much about my health because I was surely invincible. I could lie, through every action, and claim that I was a genuine male. While inside, my soul cried in longing for different textures, for compassion and under-standing, for that kind of processing unique to lesbians, for all the countless little ways women are what they are. Without the language for it, I was forced to believe that I was simply imagining things. That everyone felt as unfulfilled as I did when they looked in the mirror or beheld their interior life, that all men were hollow, shapes and nothing more.

60

My friends in college were pretty much all straight, because I figured I had to be straight even though I knew I wasn't.

My colleagues in the creative writing program were all trannies, sluts, dykes, and homos.

61

If I could not write of New York I wouldn't, but without doing so my confession is in-
complete.

I arrived at the age of 26, sober-ish, smaller and more feminine in body than I had ever
been before, a conceited little shit convinced of his own magnificence, and left huge,
broken, a wreck of my own making, ashamed of my own queerness, more ashamed of
my multiple counts of sexual harassment, and really I think that's all there is to say on the
matter.

Tiger Woods fell from grace in 2009, the year I started drinking in earnest. The two are entirely unconnected.

63

In 2009 it was reported that Tiger Woods had been involved in a car accident. Drugs may or may have not been involved, but an unnecessary detail was emphasized, that Elin Nordegren, the wife of Tiger Woods, had helped him from the car.

Over the next few days and weeks it came to light that the accident had been the result of a domestic dispute in the happy home, which resulted from Tiger Woods's massive infidelities. He had fucked his way through a seemingly countless number of women and when confronted by Elin he somehow managed to drive his car into a tree. Don't ask me how.

K was incredibly sad when Tiger Woods was revealed to be a philanderer.
It meant that the legacy of Tiger Woods would be tarnished.

He would no longer be the greatest, and in some ways K felt like all that work she had put into becoming like him was for nothing, that perhaps if she had succeeded she too would have just been a philanderer with a tarnished legacy who had to go through humiliation and divorce and watch their career slip into near oblivion just as they were on the precipice of completion.

65

My mother once made me take off my clothes so she could take Polaroids of my pubescent fatness. We waited together at the kitchen table for the photos to develop, white giving way to faint, washed out browns and yellows, the black of my hair coming in first.

Upon viewing the shots, it was clear to me that I was not, and never had been, a boy at all.

66

It took me getting sober to finally realize that what I was experiencing, the essential wrongness I could not find words for, was gender dysphoria. I was dancing in my underwear, getting ready for my shift at the big box store I worked at in Seattle. And as I danced, no mirrors, nothing to reflect my reality, I felt like something else.
I felt like a woman.

And I had felt the something-else-ness countless times over my life. I just happened to have words for it. I don't know why they came to me then. Maybe my brain was no longer soaked with counterfeit enlightenment.

To say that I was born a woman when I appear, by every metric, by every observable fact, to have been born male is quite a thing for me to claim. I do not find it a simple thing to explain or rationalize. I respect anyone who is confused by my being such, even as I rebuke those who tell me I am not.

Curiosity and ignorance are healed by knowledge, but knowing anything to a certainty breeds ignorance.

So then maybe I do not know that I am a woman. Maybe I feel it, or live as such, or am struggling to approximate my existence and summarizing it to the best of my ability. It does not make me less of what I am, any more than to know you are what you have been assigned is a panacea against doubt and deliberation. What creeps through the gaps at the edge of consciousness is fearful indeed.

68

What would you rather call me? Faggot, cross dresser, drag queen, sissy, femboy, shemale, autogynephile, choose your word, I'll take them all. They are all words which mean "woman-like" and that is the highest validation you can offer.

Truly, women are hated, and to be like a woman is perhaps the worst thing you can be, especially a low woman, a bitch, breed sow, dick wash. But that is what I am, and if I am not, or if you refuse to allow me to be that, if you must redefine it yourself, then I assure you the word you will choose instead will mean the same thing.

69

The women who reject me do so by calling me masculine, in an attempt to reverse the hatred, to artificially create misandry, that most summoned of boogeymen which still lives only in fever dreams.

What they hate is that I am not masculine. It is the incongruity. That I am woman-like, and too much, reaching too far. It is the same hatred of women that drives this, an endless howl of slurs, the denigration of knuckles, throats, legs, shoulders, to ridicule the performance or the feminine done inexpertly, to make me a bad woman, low woman, bitch, breed sow, dick wash.

And it continues until it reaches such a pitch that other women, born women, place a hand upon the shoulder, are you all right, is there something you wish to speak about, have you called your mother lately.

70

What a woman is to me: Not a womb, not a breeder, not a fuck doll, not morale gear, not eye candy, not a thing to be consumed or used or spent up, not a caretaker, not a mother, not a saint, not a servant or cook or cleaner, a woman is luminous, heavy, soft, worn, powerful, open, denigrated, despised, beloved, a human being with two X chromosomes except when not, a human being who will give birth except when she won't, a human being with a vagina except maybe not, a human being with estrogen except when she can't make it or can't afford it, long hair, short hair, body hair, no hair, teeth crooked or straight, brown skin, white skin, black skin, blacker than onyx, blacker than love, a pulse, a breath, a declaration of womanhood, a condemnation to womanhood, always a blessing of womanhood, celibate, a fuck machine, someone who lets me cry on them, likes to spit on other women during sex, someone who I let cry on me, sits down to pee, sits down to shit, someone who is reading and angry at this description, the opposite of a wound, my mother, my enemies, maybe the only people who ever loved me, and not a man.

I used to think I was nonbinary until I met my partner whom I hope to marry and realized I have no fucking idea what nonbinary means.

72

In 2019 Tiger Woods won the Masters Tournament. It was his first major tournament win in eleven years.

It is impossible for me to know this without feeling a certain amount of hope. It is a license for optimism.

It is the possibility that everything will be alright in the end.

73

My father taught me one thing that I will never not cherish.
No condition is permanent.

Things will continue to change, for better and worse.
Transform.

74

My partner whom I hope to marry is not M but is also not F and sometimes they make me think F and sometimes they make me think M even though they insist what they are is neither, and when I think of them as M I feel guilty at how much I enjoy it, how much it fits, how much I appreciate those parts of them which are seemingly obscured from them.

They sometimes fuck me like they're F except when they fuck me like they're M but what they really are is neither and that's how they usually fuck me, like a system designed to have an orgasm, something practical like they are, except here "practical" makes me think less of M or F and more like human sexuality in general, like they are sex personified, and those are times I think of them as neither and those are the times I just want to shove my fingers into them and rub myself against their leg and come with them, on them, near them, and those are the times it's the best I've ever had and I hope God is watching us, touching herself, pleased with what she's made.

I think they want their driver's license to say X.

LOVELESS

When he tells his Big Ex that he met someone, she laughs.

It doesn't matter where in New York they meet, but they don't meet on Tinder. This is a classic meet-cute.

She is 22, he is almost 30. He is skinny-fat and probably white but doesn't have to be. He is a poet or photographer who studied English or Music. She is a metalworker or essayist who studied Comparative Lit or Gender Studies. They have mutual friends and never go to the same bars.

He has an appeal, not ugly but not Hollywood or even Sundance. He doesn't go to the gym, but if he does he's not a protein powder, Alpha Male, stock-option Republican. He wears graphic tees and his hair is messy, unlike everyone else's.

She is not conventionally attractive, but (this is important!) she is not conventionally un-attractive either. She has an undercut, bangs or a half-shaved head and she wears a lot of dark colors. She is not a gym-goer. She is white, and if not she's Korean, and if not then Lebanese, but he makes an effort not to ask or comment about her ethnicity even though he wants to know. He wanted to talk to Blonde Friend or Leggy and European. He will tell himself that it's because he likes quirky, not because he is settling. She talked to him because of his funny and nonspecific sexual charisma.

She wears Forever 21. He shops at thrift stores. She drinks chai lattes, he drinks black coffee, she drinks cider, he drinks whiskey. He asks if she likes Edith Wharton, she says yeah. He says he's a feminist. He won't say he wants to fuck her. She kind of wishes he'd get it over with.

They will hang out, at parks or museums, but they won't go on dates. They will hash out the usual questions of family and occupation, while laughing at how typical these questions are. They are unconventional people doing conventional things.

When he tells his Big Ex that he is seeing someone, she says, *That's not a good idea.*

During his worn and shiny monologue, he says marriage is a capitalist institution designed to keep women in bondage by treating them as property, wherein domesticity and child-rearing are handled while the man is left free to pursue career and conquest, relegating women to second-class citizens. He says all of this in a copious breath while she tries to eat a Japanese-fusion quiche with nori and raw salmon he insisted they try.

She wants to get married, but ignores his conversation and refuses a green tea mochi ice cream taco.

He shows her his vinyl collection so she fucks him to make him stop talking. He's goofy but earnest and book smart, and if she never fucked anyone goofy she'd never fuck anyone. His breathing is too heavy and his head game is sloppy but he's good enough. He doesn't kick her out even though she leaves. He makes sure to say he wants to see her again. He texts to make sure she got home alright.

When he tells his Big Ex that he fucked someone she says, *Well, that's too bad.*

When he talks about her she's beautiful, never hot. He will not give sexual specifics. I really like her, he says. I think this might be something.

She talks to friends about Shakira and Roxanne Gay. She demands her life pass the Bechdel test. She throws herself into work, eats croissants or berries, and drinks kombucha.

When they ask about him, she says he doesn't seem like a creep. She describes his dick when they ask, in detail. Critiques his sexual performance. She defends his awful text messages. He's kind of an underachiever, she says. I still like him though..

She shows up at his job and brings him a donut. They kiss in public now. They stay over.

She is emotionally unavailable and has trust issues. He is unsure of his future and willing to take it slow.

They have a soundtrack. They have a favorite restaurant (It's not the fusion place.) They compromise on the cider/beer question by always keeping wine around. They go clubbing, or eat brunch and walk around Central Park on Sundays. They take road trips. They smoke American Spirits even though they don't smoke.

When he tells his Big Ex that he has a new girlfriend, she asks, *Does she know what you're like?*

They show each other their art. She likes his and says so. He finds hers childish and derivative yet says he loves it.

He gets sad. He goes on long self-loathing rants after he's been drinking, or they haven't had sex in a couple days. She tells him he might benefit from therapy. She tries to be there for him but it's exhausting.

She cries at random, won't talk to him for days at a time. He is tearing holes in her mental defenses. Sometimes she stares at a wall or TV. Her center of gravity has always been shifting. She doesn't even want to think about it and doesn't, except in her bed, or the bath, and maybe the library.

She goes to therapy, or went to therapy, and maybe she's medicated but probably not.

She tells him, about the boy when she was 14, 16, 18. Who was an old friend she trusted or an acquaintance, and how it was at his place or another's place. How that boy smoked her out, got her drunk, or waited till she fell asleep, and maybe just got right on top of her. When she said no that boy went along and took what he desired, as she wondered dimly if she was going to die, trapped under someone who said *I just can't help myself baby.*

She finally made it home and took a shower, didn't tell anyone for two days and never pressed charges so of course lots of people don't believe her. She lost a bunch of friends over it.

When he tells his Big Ex that his new girl was raped, she says, *You shouldn't be telling me this, you fucking weirdo.*

She doesn't tell him the details, how much it hurt, if she bled, if that boy came and if so where, three days of late-period induced terror, how she threw up watching Girl With A Dragon Tattoo, right there in the theater.

He holds her when she starts crying and says how sorry he is. He thinks of course, all these art girls have been raped. After all, one in three women have been raped. He's hoping this hasn't adversely colored her view of men, that when he chokes or slaps her in bed it doesn't bring back bad memories, that what his friends have said about sexual promiscuity among damaged women isn't true.

He holds her and repeats practiced words, so she thinks he gives a shit and falls a little extra in love with him.

When he tells his Big Ex that his new girl is moving in with him, she says, *Oh my god, the poor thing.*

She washes socks and cooks dinner more than he does but she tells herself he'll get there. He comes home and plants himself before the TV. He doesn't read as much as he claimed to. He wakes up late then runs around, cursing loudly before slamming the door.

She doesn't put her bras/jeans in the laundry hamper. She leaves dishes in the sink. Make-up rests upon the tiny bathroom sink. Her books are all over the floor and mixed with his. Sometimes he comes home and she's crying to Tori Amos.

She gives him the silent treatment by accident, finds out he's talking to his Big Ex. He's angry because she checked his phone. He watches more porn than she does. It's less rough than hers. She stares at the women's bodies, all conventionally attractive, bolt-on tits, but all with piercings or tattoos. She wonders if she's just a type to him.

He tells her she's paranoid, he's not really talking to anyone else, that hated coworkers aren't really out to get her, the creepy guy next door isn't really leering at her. He thinks she's crazy but would never say that.

When he drinks he gets angry, about dishes, books, money, and her fucking underwear. He hates her friends, always down for Chelsea but not Bushwick, how old they make him feel. He breaks glass and cuts his hand when he cleans it up, so the blood mixes with it in garbage bags. People pass their sidewalk fights, eyes averted. They call each other assholes.

He claims to have no male role models. His father never liked him, he was bad at sports. The other kids called him a faggot, which would be okay if he was, but he isn't. He sat alone in his room, stoned, playing Zelda or Halo. His first girlfriend cheated on him, and his dad told him that's what women do. Maybe his dad used to beat his mom, or yell with brown-liquor breath.

He's not the one saying those things, it's his father, maybe also his basketball coach, but he still doesn't know how to treat women.

Baby, you just need to be patient.

He promises he'll get therapy but never does.

One day he punches a hole in the wall and that's it. 9, 12, 18 months gone and done with. He begs her to stay but she threatens to call the police. She stays with a friend. She double checks with their mutuals so she won't see him in public.

She cries to friends and gets drunk. He cries alone and gets drunk. She starts accepting Xanax from friends. He starts accepting cocaine from strangers. She fucks an ex she'd started up with a month before the break up. He fucks a coworker he'd been texting the whole time.

When he tells his Big Ex that they broke up, she asks, *Did you cheat on her? Did you hit her too?*

Then come his many texts. She won't answer at first. They meet for coffee and he apologizes. She says she forgives him. She doesn't. They meet a few other times but she doesn't want to be around him, doesn't feel safe. He hopes they'll get back together, realizes the impossibility weeks later.

She swears it will never happen again. Maybe even swears off guys entirely.

He swears it will never happen again. He self-loathes and remakes the narrative.

They both write about the relationship. His thinkpiece is called, *What Not to Do When You Meet The Love of Your Life, or What My Father Taught Me About Women.*

Hers is called, *Gaslighting: It Can Happen to You, or I Let You Get to Me, or Loveless.*

He never calls her crazy. He's a feminist. Instead he calls her troubled and difficult, and too good for him.

She doesn't call him abusive. She's too kind. She tells her friends he was fucked up and really sad and just not mature enough for a relationship.

Maybe she goes to rehab, probably not. He doesn't. They learn language to put to their experience. They re-enter the dating pool.

They spiral away from each other into new arrangements. The same type, but different words. She says upfront that she craves stability, wants to be married.
He doesn't take anyone to the Japanese fusion place.

They can see the patterns, move in spaces already cut out for them by those who came before. The vestments have changed but the body remains. They are no longer victim or monster. Those words have dried out.

RETREAT

We arrived Friday afternoon. I rode down with my sponsor and their roommate. When they talked of God I nodded in the rearview. Nobody knew I had lost my faith.

The organizers placed me in a cabin with three men even though I identified as a woman. It wasn't the worst thing but it did make me wish that I could be in the women's world where I more clearly belonged. The hormones had already begun to take their toll and I had visible breasts and less body hair and my hairline was creeping back down my skull. I think the organizer put me there because my sponsor identifies as a man, and it was tradition for sponsees to crash with their sponsors.

Our cabin was across the clearing from my partner's cabin. My partner would break up with me directly after the retreat. They would say, they didn't believe they could have the kind of sobriety their sponsor had so long as they were with me. I was not aware of this.
They strung their cabin with pink lights and pink flamingos trotted on the grass in front. There was a competition for best cabin. They were in the lead.

At night there was a meeting around a campfire after dinner. We read the preamble and steps and prayed and then took turns sharing. We were only supposed to smoke in one designated area near the parking lots but that didn't stop us from surreptitiously burning squares as we sat on stumps, back cold, front too hot. Someone passed around a bag of lavender and after each share we threw a handful onto the fire.

It was lovely and did nothing to restore my faith in God.

In the cthonic gloom of the clearing, my partner's cabin was a Pepto-Bismol conflagration. Even so, it was as if the pines wouldn't allow any light to go too far. It was only a twinkle, and I felt very far away. We didn't decorate our cabin.

When I squeezed myself into my sleeping bag the lights were still there, dancing around our cabin, impossibly weaving their way on the bottom of my sponsor's bunk, struggling vainly against the all-encompassing darkness.

The voice of God, who I did not believe in, spoke to me in the darkness. Your every misfortune will have its opposite. I stopped worrying and fell asleep, lulled by the pink lights.

RAT
FUCK

Plague rats running rampant sickening people crawling one on top the other. the city is prettiest when she's ill. I could write forever and never get there.

Last night I heard helicopters waiting patiently with rotary wings looking for signs of life. Squash it out with a bang bang no more rats here sir.

We could die like this, I want to die in the suburbs searching for a sign of intelligent life, but instead I have to step over homeless people on my way into the section 8.

The rats will turn on and eat each other and I'm not even a rat, I'm a flea making apologies going from snout to tail, farm to table saying I'm sorry, I apologize, please forgive my existence.

Fleas do well. Fleas get fat and are upwardly mobile. Fleas enjoy a high standard of living. Everyone hates a flea.

Hate turns inward turns sickening manufactured and out of place. Hate what kills you not what you live on. I hate god for making me like this. I would like to take this moment to pray.

SANGUINISTA

Katherine eases herself into the too-warm water and grimaces. The clinic volunteer gave her one pill of mifepristone (RU-486) and four pills of misoprostol. She washed them down with brunch mimosas and two Vicodin. Her phone, resting on the edge, vibrates, displays a name: Maria.

I want to keep it, he had said. As if her years were his, as if her dissertations and grants, her future beach house could be claimed.

She was not prepared for the medicine-induced red flood that soaked up three large tampons and the thickest pad she could find. The cramping was like every period she had ever had at once.

Katherine has returned to Corydon, IN because she didn't want to have to deal with his incessant nagging. He would feign care and continue to insist she take his check. Concern would decay into the sticky black guilt of manipulation. The risk that he would take this termination as a favor is too great. This must be a selfish act.

The steaming water is pink like the teddy bear she threw away, a gift from her first lover. Her name was Amber. They'd been 14. It had been an indiscretion: her parents were Presbyterian. Corydon is not kind. There has been violence. A precious bleeding lip, care of a homophobic bully. Katherine's own mother laughed it off as a phase. Her father was already dead of heroin, so no one consulted him.

I'll help you take care of it. I'll ask for a promotion. He would tie her to Bloomington. She'd be the wife of a townie, waiting for her husband to come home from slinging pizzas to trust fund college sophomores with adult braces.

Now it's crimson. Maria calls again. She's surprised at the rate of flow, but more angry about the pain. Reflexively, she casts forward through memory. She must not think of Maria, of her lost island of serenity. One pain is enough for now.

In New York she dated a conceptual artist named River who incessantly talked about their vagina. Katherine assumed they were also on scholarship. She had found them charming until she realized political messaging obscured River's lax talents. River's housemate Esther was a law student, a better lay, and a superior artist. River blamed the breakup on internalized misogyny, but the truth is their piece involving "hillbillies" didn't square with River's family-financed Williamsburg brownstone. Katherine saw images of Esther's last gallery showing a week ago. Photographs of working mothers and lost teens she works with.
My parents can help us out. The idea of marriage is itself loathsome. Can't he see this is an incident, not an opportunity? An inconvenience.

Her feet are almost obscured under reddened clouds. The water is cooling, still warm enough for a modicum of relief. She will take what small comfort she can. Paige was during Katherine's fully-funded Masters in London. She eventually left and started a family with a very kind Syrian engineer with a great beard. The two events were not connected. Katherine doesn't often think of Paige because they left on good terms, with respect and appreciation.

Dyke cunt. She's heard it so often it doesn't register. Straight men are boring in their cruelty.

The waters have darkened. What made Maria so perfect was that she asked so little. There was space. Maria only shaved her legs on Wednesdays. Her biology research was incomprehensible to Katherine but the music in her voice was pleasing. Maria would listen to paragraphs about Joan Didion and Lil' Kim. She would cook rice and black beans and shame Katherine for not cleaning the spicy chicken bones, call her a gringo and ask if she was ever hungry, then cry when Katherine spoke, quietly, of the trailer park and her mother's valiant Tuna Helper innovations. They are no longer together, but they cannot bear to be apart.

You made me do that. She doesn't have the words for it. He calls the beating a mistake. She agrees, mostly. He has cured her of queerness, as he said he would. She's just a lesbian, now.

She spasms in her own blood. The phone vibrates again and falls in the tub and Katherine scrambles to retrieve it, cursing. When she pulls it out of the red, it won't turn on. It is only now, having lost the one thing she wanted to keep, that she can summon the energy to scream.

PHYSICAL SYMPTOMS
OF DEPRESSION

Include: Oversleeping, like you did when no one wanted to take you to prom. When you couldn't get a job out of college. And now, when your career has stalled.

Other symptoms. Undereating. I brought home rented DVDs of your favorite films and the jalapeño chips you like. I got your favorite dumplings from the place on Henry Street. The therapist says that a Loving Significant Other can be enormously helpful. I'm not angry, but it's too bad that I spent on all this food.

Can you die of depression-induced starvation?

Would you like to find out?

Joint and muscle pain. You blame the 9 straight days stocking beauty supplies and condoms. Please consider that, given your relative youth, the aches are exasperated by other factors.

As you have told me many times, there is no cure for depression.

Crying is a symptom. To get technical, the sorrow is the symptom. But it manifests, as we see here, in snot and tears.

Disappointment is a physical symptom of depression, but only when that disappointment is made real via abandoning very fine paints and brushes, purchased by a Loving S/O. This creates a void in your creative output. Which is why you haven't had a show in years.

Suicide is not a physical symptom of depression. It is an ineffective, do it yourself treatment.

You laughed when I told you this. It is so rare to see you laugh, and all the lovelier for it. Anhedonia. This is the lack of feeling. Emotional and mental. Physical. You no longer get the little hit of dopamine that comes with eating a tasty dumpling.

Or fucking your wealthy, very fit, Loving S/O.

While anhedonic, you describe the sensation as being "hollow" in both mind and flesh. A body with the organs pulled out. This state is, as far as you are concerned, indiscernible from death. This is why I keep certain medications and sharp objects on lockdown.

This state can last for a weekend. Or the entire month of February, after opening a rejection letter. While in this state, you may administer stimulants such as cocaine and Adderall to alleviate the symptoms. More commonly alcohol, marijuana, and Vicodin are used as anesthetics.

Intoxication is not a physical symptom of depression.

Both conventional wisdom and your therapist hold that a healthy relationship with your Loving S/O can be a baseline for further growth and treatment. This is why I have refrained from speaking this frankly in the past. But it's been a week, and you haven't moved.

Perhaps I'm not a Loving S/O. Am I your spouse, or your lover? Best friend? A narrative construction of your illness? A fuck buddy? A counterfeit?

The dumplings are beginning to congeal.

When you told me of your illness I assumed it would be mild. You could smoke a little weed, lift some weights. Deep breathing. Yoga. Not endless pill bottles. Definitely not scars.

Can you hear me? I am not speaking aloud. You cannot hear me. If you could, then I would not speak. I would be crueler.

Physical symptoms of depression include: your Loving S/O disappearing in the middle of the night.

There's no saving these dumplings.

It has occurred to me that the purpose of a Loving S/O is not to dote upon you. It is impossible to fuck or feed you out of this state. My purpose is merely to occupy space.

There is no living thing I wouldn't kill to save you.

But the blood of virgins, as you told me, is not an effective treatment.

I will sit in silence for as long as you need me to. If it is possible to die of starvation like this, we will find out together. I am your Loving S/O. There is no cure for depression.

MANIA
SEASON

You lend me a hundred dollars to get drunk because you say you want to have fun with me and part of me wants you to know how much that sounds like i'm your lover but you're straight all american good old salt of the earth boy so you'd think i was joking we start out in greenwood with moscow mules then we move down to columbia city to drink beers and watch the mariners game with your cousin then we wander around and take the light rail back up to capitol hill and we drink at the unicorn until they close then we want to go to lost lake but the line is too long so we wander through cal anderson park i steal an abandoned handy grabber you start playing in the fountain we take an uber home and you don't like how i ask the driver to drive us up the hill so you get really mad and go off and tell me how rude i am and that you can kick me out of your apartment even though we are both on the lease and i tell you to leave me the fuck alone and i go in my room and try to close the door and you won't let me you keep pounding on the door trying to get in pound pound pound you are shirtless and angry and terrify me you are so hot all american good old salt of the earth boy and finally you leave me alone and go in your room and when i wake up the next day you're gone but you left me a note saying you were gonna go watch the mariners game and i never drink again.

SHAGGING FLIES
IN BALLARD

I resolve to confess my feelings on Saturday. You take me to the batting cage up in Mount-lake Terrace but the machines are so awful they eat our tokens and give us nothing back, no high-arching softballs or baseball bullets. I would never say anything because I am meek and unmasculine but you get a refund because you are handsome and friendly and always get what you want and I am jealous—of your confidence and looks and talents and physicality and how much sex you have.

There's a bucket of baseballs in your trunk so we drive to a park in Ballard and grab the bats and bucket and I'm way out of shape and can't pitch for shit. You whack more than a few out into the home run range and we shag them together and take turns, pitcher and hitter, the innuendo not lost on me though you are oblivious to it, as I admire your form and feel a certain kind of carefree peace and joy, just two guys hitting baseballs, and it makes me wish you were my boyfriend in a way I find embarrassing, and I will tell you, hyper-straight you, college-baseball-player you, writer you, talented-in-more-than-every-way you.

This isn't the right moment to say anything because it's too perfect, as if I have already gotten exactly what I want, and having had it, there is no reason for me to seek it.

We catch the Mariners game at a pizza place and you drink a beer while I drink a Diet Coke because I'm scared of what comes out of me while I'm drunk. You ask me how the date with that guy went and I say Fine when it wasn't fine because he wasn't you, and I don't care unless I care and you make me care in spite of myself.

We lock eyes as you say Yeah, just fine? And your voice is so warm and your eyes are crystal, your Henley revealing just a bit of your chest and I am an animal, my higher functions suspended even as I can feel your thoughts move, and I realize that this is my moment, my time to confess, and as I prepare the words Zunino blasts one and the bar goes wild and we high-five and really is it worth it to complicate a friendship when it's so much easier to let your heart break.

ZEKE

"When you're a star,
they let you do it."

- Donald Trump, 45th President of
the United States of America

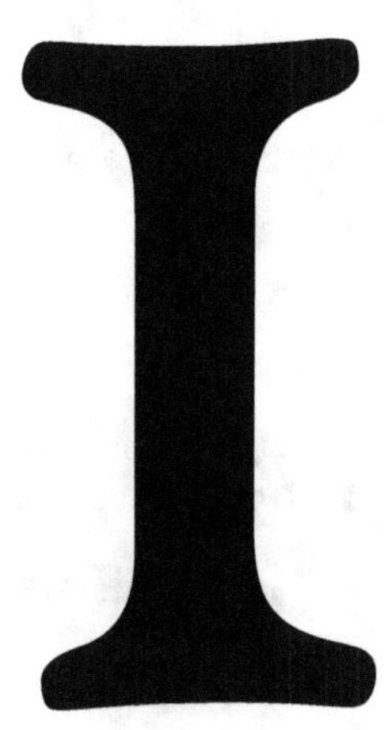

This is just in case people want to know what happened. I've got a lot of time on my hands, sitting here in grippy socks with no belt cause they think I'm going to off myself. All I'm saying is, I don't let myself get taken advantage of without some payback. *Nemo me impune lacessit.* So how about I tell it my way so at least when I get called a monster, it's clear what kind of monster I am, and so that if I die I can do so in peace?

The way I met my boyfriend was that he was being bullied.

These two assholes, Ralph and Lloyd, they were picking on the new kid, slapping his face a little, trying to pull of his beanie, calling him a faggot and slamming his books out of his hand. And I mean, the new kid was clearly a homosexual. He had a total gay vibe, kind of a mincing, lisping sort of deal, and it didn't bother me but it did bug these two hillbilly juniors and so I figured hey, yeah I'm only 14 but I'm a pretty big guy, so I went up to Ralph and I slammed him against the lockers.

"What the fuck?"

"Quick picking on him," I said.

Well, I don't know what I expected, but he shoved me back and I swung on him and landed a good one but then Lloyd kicked me in the shins and knocked me one across the jaw that damn near took me out, but it got some steel in the new kid's spine so he started fighting back, and it kept going until the soccer coach came by and broke it up and sent us to the principal's office.

The new kid, Ben, he was looking pretty bloodied while we waited for the principal but I reached over and told him my name was Zeke and that he wouldn't have to worry about the hillbillies anymore, I'd keep an eye on them.

Ben said, "Thanks," and shook my hand, real limp like, but I didn't mind it. He had pretty hazel eyes and this shaggy black haircut and I thought he was cute even though or maybe because he had blood on his face. The effect was kind of pleasing. He could stand up for himself too, given a bit of a push, and that was an appealing quality as well.

Me, I think I scared him. I'm big for my age, big as in tall and also broad, and my voice is kind of deep, and everyone assumes I'm like 18 when they meet me.

But anyway, we got to the principal's office and all four of us got suspended, which wouldn't go down well with my old man I know, but it's not like I really cared all that much. He's an uppity asshole from Milwaukee who moved us out to Kentucky for some kind of job to do with seeds. Apparently genetic engineering pays well, cause we've got a nice house in a subdivision and two BMWs and everything and my mom doesn't even have to work besides giving out piano lessons to church kids.

I asked if he wanted to hang out after school and he said sure and that we could go to his place. "My dad won't care. He'll probably be stoned."

"Must be nice to have chill parents."

"No. I hate him. All he does is smoke weed and he never took care of me or my siblings. They don't talk to him now."

I nodded. I still thought it sounded cool to have a weed-smoking dad who didn't ride your ass over grades or church attendance or tell you to pull up your pants or turn your damn rock music down.

"Where's your mom?"

"Dead. Died of an overdose."

"Sorry."

So after we got suspended I went to his house and his dad wasn't even home. We went up to his room which was covered in all kinds of posters featuring weird symbols that my parents would definitely think were demonic. There was a tank with a black and white snake inside in the corner.

"Cool snake."

"Thanks. I have to feed him, actually. Hang on."

He left me alone in the room for a second and so I did some more looking around. A lot of his stuff, clothes, sheets, furniture, was black and what wasn't was like purple or dark blue or electric green. None of it matched and the place was kind of a mess and didn't smell too good. I know they say teenagers aren't very neat but I like to keep my things very straightened out and put together. It's just the way I've always been.

He came back with this dead white rat. He reached into the cage and took the snake out and put it in a bin sitting near the cage, and then he dropped the rat into the bin. The snake went for it immediately.

"What's his name?"

"Midgard."

I thought, just for a moment, that it was a shame the rat was dead. I would have liked to see it struggle as the snake inevitably destroyed it.

Ben grabbed his computer and we sat on the bed. He asked what kind of music I listened to.

"90's rock."

"Oh okay. I don't know if you'd like my music.

"Let me hear some."

He played a song for me and it was this ungodly noise, just these electronic bleeps and like sampled angle grinder sounds over what I assume were meant to be drums. He told me it was called aggrotech and I nodded. It wasn't bad, it was just weird, but I kind of liked it and besides I obviously liked him so I wasn't going to like, tell him that I wasn't the biggest fan of whatever he liked.

"I make tracks too. Hang on." He played me one of his own and it was more chill, down tempo, with a decent groove, and I told him it was like way better than the first song and he laughed and blushed. He was on SoundCloud under the name Killer Heaven and I said I would totally follow him if I had a SoundCloud.

He laughed again and I reached over and kissed him on the mouth and he let me so I kissed him again and then kind of tackled him down to the sheets and made out with him and it was honestly really nice. Ben is a good kisser.

He had all these scars on his thighs and upper arms that I knew were from cutting himself. I asked how long ago it had been since he'd done it and he said it was like over a year. I made him promise he wouldn't do it again. Cutting yourself is a bad habit.

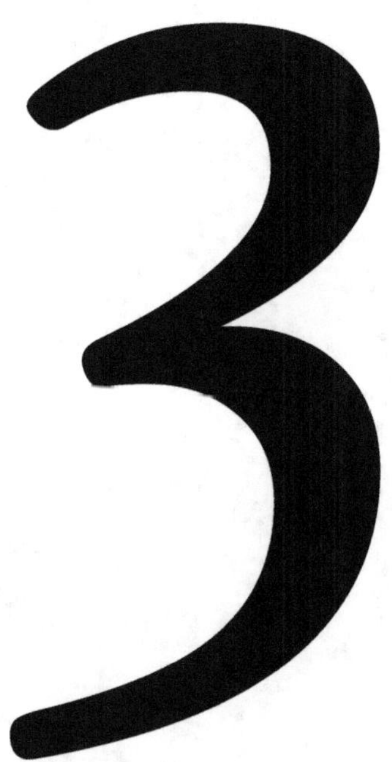

I gave my uncle a heart attack because he wouldn't stop molesting me. I would go over there while my parents had date night and then one night while I was playing Call of Duty he started touching me and reached into my pants.

He told me not to tell anyone or I'd be in trouble, because he'd say I came on to him, so I didn't really have much of a choice if I wanted him to stop, which of course I did. I really did think about telling someone but he was probably right about how they would have blamed me. People are always blaming me for things that aren't my fault.

He liked to shoot meth, because he was a druggie as well as a pedo. But he also had arthritis and was no good at hitting veins anymore. He'd picked up the meth thing late in life. So what he would do was, he would have me mix up the shot and stick it in him. Eventually he didn't even watch me measure out how much I gave him, which is why it was so easy for me to mix up like five times his usual dose and give his kid-raping ass a heart attack.

At first I couldn't believe it as I watched him fall off his chair and hit the floor. But as soon as he stopped moving I knew I'd pulled it off. The guy had a bad ticker anyway so it wasn't like they were going to look for evidence of an overdose. I flushed the dope and the needles and called 911, doing my best to fake a good cry, which wasn't really necessary cause I guess I was so quiet and pale when my parents and the paramedics got there that everyone just assumed I was in shock.

I know I should feel bad that I killed him, but I really don't. I strongly believe he deserved it. *Nemo me impune lacessit.* Who knows how many other kids he fucked? I don't know what he did the other 29 days out of the month besides my parents' date night. I'm glad he's dead. I think there's too many people on Earth as it is. We need another plague.

That's how I got stuck with this piece of shit shrink that I hate. I straight up told her that I killed him, like I got so bored and tired of listening to her talk that I explained, in detail, just like I did here, how I killed the old fuck, and you know what she said? I suffer from delusions brought on by grief. She didn't believe me! How do you like that, I tell someone I committed a murder and they shrug it off like "No, you didn't."

She said it was clear, it was obvious that he had died of a natural heart attack, that he had been overweight and a smoker and that it wasn't all that inconceivable for someone his age to die suddenly, and that I was full of shit, basically. I couldn't believe it, but I just went along with it because how lucky can you get? She prescribed me some medication and sent me on my way, and I just figured fuck it, why not.

People call me a liar all the time, and I guess that's just cause they can't deal with the truth. Like the principal, who said I attacked those two redneck motherfuckers unprovoked when he knew they were picking on Ben. She's full of shit, is what I'll tell you. I stuck up for the gay kid and he just didn't want to admit that I was in the right. She'd rather defend those Trump fanboys than take a stand against them, because she's weak.

Me, I don't have a problem telling them to fuck off. I think it's what they deserve, at the very least. Trump supporters aren't people, they're meatbags that shouldn't get to breathe the same air as the rest of us. They ruin everything they touch, and they're annoying. I don't really get into politics, I just know I can't stand them, and I think that's enough of an opinion to have.

Called it on my dad being pissed about the suspension, but not pissed enough to ground me or whatever. I told him straight up that it wasn't my fault, that I had been trying to defend someone weaker than me, but he still told me I would have to talk to the pastor, as if I wanted anything to do with that old bastard. The way he looks at me creeps me out. That smile. Disgusting.

I went up to my room and checked out Ben's SoundCloud. He had a lot of followers, which surprised me, but then again it didn't cause he was pretty good.

So I met with the old fuck the next Sunday after service. He preaches what I think is like, prosperity gospel shit? That we can all be rich and fruitful and all that if only we can turn ourselves towards God and go with his will. I'm not an expert on the God thing, I don't really care about it and my parents don't push it very hard, they just want me to go to church and hope I soak it up somehow. I'm secretly an atheist, like I think religion is violent and bad and just exists to separate people from their money.

After the service the pastor told me that fighting wasn't the Christian thing to do and that we ought to seek peaceful solutions to our problems, which was a crock of shit for reasons I don't have to list out here. Yeah, how many Crusades were there again? Spare me.

He told me that God didn't want me starting fights, that Christ told us to turn the other cheek and that it was best to, I guess, just lay there and take it. That I should trust bigger and stronger people would sort everything out, even if it didn't make sense at the time.

I asked him, "But what about trying to help an innocent?"

He was kind of stumped but he said that what I should have done was get an adult, instead of directly intervening. Which is its own pile of crap. What was an adult going to do in that situation? Those hillbillies needed their noses bloodied. They needed to get their asses whooped a little bit, for the sake of Ben if nobody else. Like I was going to sit there and let him get hate crimed by a couple of inbred punks.

The pastor sensed my resistance and asked me if there was anything else I wanted to tell him. Then he reached over to me and put a hand on my knee and slowly slid it up my thigh, and then he smiled that horrible grin. He told me he'd give me his number and I'd just have to text him, whenever I felt like I needed to talk. Better yet, he said, how about I give him my number, and he could check in with me sometime?

That's when I realized that I was going to kill this guy.

Dad took us out to Bob Evans with another family afterwards and we prayed over the food. The other family's got like six kids which is way too many. They don't believe in birth control, so the father just fucks his wife and every year like clockwork they pump out another kid. My parents don't believe in birth control either, but there was something wrong with my mom's uterus and they had to remove it. You can tell she wanted more kids besides me. She had three miscarriages before I was born. That wears on a person. I love her and want her to be happy but I can't help but be thankful I'm an only child.

Six goddamn kids is too many kids. People shouldn't be allowed to breed as it is. Kids don't consent to be born, it's unethical to make more of them. If I had the chance to not be born you best believe I would take the sweet oblivion of having never been.

Anyway, the waiter who took care of us initially was gay. Like, drag queen gay, too-gay-to-live gay. I'm always surprised by how many open cocksuckers there are in this town. Well, my dad wasn't having that, so he called over the manager and asked for a different server, so we got some fat bitch to help us instead.

The other dad at the table piped up "Well, he did take a long time to bring us coffee."

"Oh, was that it, dad?" I wanted to hear him say it, I don't know why. Probably because I hate myself.

"Ezekiel," said my mother in warning.

I nodded, like it was the most reasonable thing in the world, and when the fat bitch swung back around to take our order I got eggs benedict, the gayest thing on the menu, and when we left I locked eyes with the gay waiter and made sure he knew that I was sorry.

Okay but get this: Ralph and Lloyd? They left Ben alone after the incident, because violence works whether people want to admit it or not. They weren't scared so much as it didn't seem worth it to mix it up with a kid that they'd already got suspended over once. That or they got bored, I don't know. I'm just glad they left him alone. The only problem was then they started saying I was his boyfriend, which no one believed cause I was a big, pretty masculine dude. I should have been playing football but I didn't care about sports, the only like athletic thing I do is work out pretty regularly, lift weights, run. Academics and art have always been more my thing.

I like books. I'm not going to put a bunch of them in a list over here so I can impress anybody, but I do like books and I read them outside of class. I like movies too, in fact I've thought about doing film in college if I don't do like literature or history or something, or maybe I'll listen to my dad and become an engineer. But what I really like to do is go online and download movies that are real fucked up, like super violent or sexual, and I watch those. The most fucked up I've seen is Guinea Pig 2 which is like this kind of fake snuff film where a dude in samurai gear chops up this girl in a basement. There's like no plot. It's really gross and I don't think it's a very good movie but it is like an endurance thing, like the kind of thing you'd watch on a dare.

I tried to show it to Ben but he got all freaked out and couldn't get more than like seven minutes in, which surprised me because he likes all that loud music and dark stuff but it turns out he's wimpy about gore. He prefers romance, he's that kind of a goth kid, which is fine, it's just that stuff kind of bores me and I'd rather watch Ichi the Killer or something like that than the cheesy Bram Stoker's Dracula movie he's obsessed with.

Whatever. We get along cause we both kind of like art and shit.

Guys like Ralph and Lloyd, they hate art. All they know is rebel flags and country music, and that's not art, that's ignorant trash. These kids talk about how they support Trump, how they think he's the shit, how he's going to kick all the Latinx kids out of the country. I've heard both of them yell "Build the wall" at these Mexican kids and it's the most fucked up thing, they say it's just jokes but I don't think they're joking.

Me, I like immigrants. My mom is an immigrant, yeah from Europe but still. These kids think they're so great but they had everything handed to them. Immigrants like my mom have to work at it, it ain't easy having to speak a second language every day. And it's not even like all these Latinx kids are immigrants, they're just as fucking American as I am. See, I give a shit about that but these ignorant redneck motherfuckers don't think that way.

They say it's ridiculous that people compare Trump to Hitler but I've seen the shit they send back and forth to each other, gas chamber memes and shit. Spare me. If I could I'd kill every Trump supporter that ever lived. These people are out of their damn minds.

My dad watches Fox News and the shit that comes out of that TV blows my fucking mind. I'm getting angry just thinking about it. One day my dad is going to get what's coming to him, if not from me then from somebody else.

Ben and I, at first, would just hang out at his place, just the two of us and the snake, and his dad in the other room. He'd play songs for me and I'd tell him about movies I'd watched the night before, and I'd watch him make tracks and we'd find weird fucked up videos on the internet, a lot of them just funny porno clips, and we'd laugh and eat pizza rolls and finally one of us would get up the courage to make out with the other one.

I got to meet his dad and he definitely seemed like a cool guy, as much as an adult can be a cool guy. He's a real hippie type, long hair, Grateful Dead shirt, like the works, and the first time he met me he tried to sell me an eighth of mushrooms, which I declined. I don't do drugs or drink, not because of morality but because I like to keep myself sharp. I do smoke cigarettes now and again if someone offers, which is a problem because Ben smokes these Djarum brand cigarettes that are black and smell like incense, which I actually really enjoy but I don't want to get addicted.

The dad doesn't seem like a pervert and he also asked like straight out if we were dating which made Ben blush and he didn't answer so I just mumbled something about us hanging out.

We started going out in public together. He drives this old truck his dad gave him because he's two years older than me despite being like a head shorter and weighing damn near half as much. We started going out in public, just to like arcades or Denny's or whatever, and no one would know we were a couple if they saw us, except for this one time he tried to make out with me in the parking lot of the Walmart he works at against the side of the truck and I pushed him off because I don't want anyone to know I'm gay.

He was mad cause he just got off a long shift. But the thing was that I'd had some friends drop me off at the Walmart like it was no big deal, I was going to meet Ben there, and they started giving me shit for being gay and I was like no I'm not gay and they kept it up until I punched one of them in the arm, hard, and they let up after that. It's not that I'm ashamed I just can't come out because I'm afraid of how people will react.

I tried to explain all that to Ben but he just started crying, so I grabbed him and held him close which felt really good. It's frustrating to have to keep it all inside like this and it made me hurt Ben which I really don't want to do. I held him close in the Walmart parking lot, his tears wettening my shirt, and I thought to myself under the pounding LED lights overhead that I was in love with him.

I used to use the gay cruising apps to find potential targets. I would fantasize about finding some pedo who knew I was underage, and then I would meet up with him and kill him. That was like my ultimate fantasy, to become a serial killer who exclusively dealt in pedos. But I would always chicken out when I got close, I would like arrange the meet up and then never show, or I would just block the guys as soon as they messaged "hey" or whatever. I just couldn't get my nerve up.

The pastor was a different story.

He and I started texting back and forth and it didn't take long for things to get sexual. He started asking for pictures of my ass and my cock, and told me that he wanted to watch me shower. And then he got sacrilegious, started talking about how he'd stare at me during the service and think about fucking me and how he wanted to do it with me in the sanctuary, right there on the pews, if only he could get away with it. It grossed me out but I kept texting him anyway, telling him to make sure to delete it all every night so no one would be able to see what we were talking about.

I felt bad about leading him on like that, not because he was never going to fuck me, but because it made me feel like I was being unfaithful to Ben, even if we'd only been seeing each other a couple weeks. It had gotten serious pretty fast, I think. Neither of us had a boyfriend before, he apparently moved around too much and I just had never found a worthy enough gay guy my age in this town. I don't want to be like I'm not like those other faggots but I am kind of an outcast even among gays. I'm not into drag queens and pop stars and Timothee Chalamet, but I'm not into sports and other typical guy shit either. I pretty much like working out and movies and books and shit, and I spend a lot of time online. Ben is cool because he likes weird shit too, like all this music I haven't heard of, and he reads too, like he knows who Dennis Cooper is which is rad, and he spends a lot of time online too, like we've probably run into each other on the /lit/ board of 4chan before. Not that I love 4chan anymore, it's too full of those "I'm not really a Nazi" type Nazi motherfuckers who I can't stand.

But yeah the pastor, he wanted it bad, it was terrible. He would come up to me after service those couple weeks I was stringing him along and he'd shake my hand and I could like feel the lust inside of him. I wished that I could have stuck him like a pig right then and there, but there's no way I would have gotten away with that.

I'd had guys come at me like that before, and I'd never liked it. It had always creeped me out and made me feel dirty and awful and impure, like I'd done something to bring it on even though I knew I hadn't.

But I knew, the whole time it was going down, that he'd get what was coming to him one day.

It took me the longest time to get Ben to tell me about his mom and why he'd moved to Kentucky. To be honest I kind of didn't want to know, because that was like his business and I didn't want to make him talk about something he didn't want to talk about, but he finally came out and said what happened, and it was like this.

The family had lived near Chicago and they'd been happy. Apparently the parents each made okay money, the mom was a manager at JC Penney and the dad did welding stuff. It wasn't too great, not with three kids, but they got by. Eventually though the mom broke her foot, dropped a box or something on it, and the pain pills turned into a heroin problem that got bad enough she got fired from her job and eventually overdosed one day. Apparently Ben is the one that found her.

She'd been the religious one out of the two parents, not really too much but a little bit, and he'd tried to get into spirituality after she died to carry on her memory but really it was the music that kept him going. He'd named his first digital EP after her, which I thought was really sweet.

The dad kind of went off the deep end after that and lost his job too. He started smoking a ton of weed and moved the family around, chasing after decent jobs that he never lasted more than a year at. Ben kind of wanted to get emancipated now that he was 16 and that was a thing he could do, but he still loved the old man no matter what.

His siblings, not so much. The sister got married and cut everyone off but the brother straight up hated his dad so much it was wild. They couldn't be in the same room together without getting into a fistfight.

Sometimes I feel bad for Ben having such a fucked up family. I mean, mine isn't great but it's not the worst, and I can kind of deal with all the fucked up shit they do and say. It just feels unfair that all the bad luck should have to come down on him, that it shouldn't be kind of evenly distributed sort of. That's not the way the world should be, but it's how it is, and I guess we kind of just have to deal.

Finally the pastor said he couldn't take it anymore and he had to have me, so I said okay, let's do this. I chose one of those date nights my parents now left me alone for and I told the pastor to come pick me up. I dressed nice for the occasion, even put on the jockstrap I'd procured from a sex shop that didn't card, and I got my bag together and walked to the entrance of my subdivision and waited for the pastor to arrive.

He was ten minutes late but he showed up in his white Cadillac to take me away. Our destination was a motel on the nasty side of town, the side of town my boyfriend lived on, the side the Walmart was located at.

"You look stunning," he said to me as I got in. His hand went immediately to my thigh.

I grunted "Thanks," but it was all I could do to stop myself from killing him right then and there. I admit I was nervous, after all this was a new experience I was going to have tonight.

He pulled away and the closer we got to the place the further up his hand went. He tried to put a hand down the front of my jeans but I brushed his hand away like, Not yet, I want it to be special. It turns out that I didn't have to do a whole lot of seducing to get this guy excited. Most pedos aren't interested in being romanced, they just want to nut and get it over with, not that I'd ever let them.

I waited in the car and listened to Billy Joel as he got the motel room keys. He very much didn't want anyone to see us together, a feeling that I was now familiar with because of how I was treating Ben, and realizing that just pissed me off more and made me want to complete the act more than ever, as a kind of fuck you to the universe for even putting me into this position. Like, way to make me relate to a pedo, God! I didn't even believe in a god at that point, but if I did I think he would want me to murder pedos, no matter what the Bible might have to say on the matter. Actually, if anything the Bible agreed. I mean sure, it says that regular gay guys and lesbians are perverts too, and that's fucked up, but still.

He came back with the keys and we pulled around the back to number 17A on the first floor. I snatched my bag and got out of the car and on the way to the door of the room he reached over and grabbed my ass, which again just made me want to cut off his hand.

When we got inside he sat on the bed and said, "I have a confession. I've never done this before."

"Really."

"Not with someone so, you know. Young."

I shrugged and took off my shirt. I didn't have too much hair on there so it was okay, I guess? I don't know what it is about underage boys that gets pedos off. He went over to the dresser and took something out of his pocket, something I recognized immediately.

"You like to party?" he asked.

I shook my head. "Nah, I'm good." I took off my pants and bent down to my bag as he snorted first one, then two lines of the meth off a mirror he'd brought from home. Of course. How pathetic. I shoved the switchblade into my jockstrap.

He came up for air and flopped down on the bed. I told him to take off his clothes and he did, his body pretty good for someone in their fifties, his prick a decent size but to me an abhorrent weapon. I straddled him on the bed and started to grind against him. He reached around and smacked my ass.

I was starting to have second thoughts, to be honest. I mean who does something like this?

Am I a psychopath? If I have to ask, does that mean I'm not one? It occurred to me that this guy had a wife and kids, that I'd be depriving more people than just the pastor of his life. What a cruel, fucked up thing for me to do. And maybe I wouldn't have gone through with it if he hadn't opened his mouth.

"I want to rape the shit out of you," he said.

And you know what? Hearing those words, that he knew what he was doing, that he used the proper word for it, drove me over the edge. I pulled out the blade and shoved it into his neck up to the hilt.

He immediately began to gurgle and it was clear he was trying to scream but couldn't. I pulled the blade out and started stabbing all over his chest. He tried to throw me off but I just kept going, stabbing him, fucking new holes all over his body until he finally flopped onto the saturated comforter, lifeless.

I calmly walked into the bathroom and took a shower, washing his blood down the drain as I cleaned up the mess. The switchblade I left stuck in the body but I made sure to clean off the handle so as not to leave fingerprints. I wiped the whole room down and changed my clothes, taking the bloody ones with me. I'd throw them out on the side of the highway as I walked home, and that's what I did, walked the miles home from the motel, listening to "Possum Kingdom" on repeat. I don't know why I had that song stuck in my head but I did.

10

The news of the pastor's demise ripped through town, and boy did I not have an opinion about that. It felt like everyone went to our church, all of a sudden, and don't get me wrong it was a big church, but not that big. I showed up to his viewing with my parents and looked down at his remains and wow, they did a great job cleaning up his body for the funeral so he didn't look so much like a block of Jarlsberg. I tried not to laugh when I saw him, which was weird cause I was actually really scared to see the body again.

Everyone speculated about who would kill him like that but for the longest time nobody mentioned that he was found in a motel room, naked, with a pile of meth sitting on the dresser right there. The meth was the clear giveaway that it was a gay thing, I think. Meth is a gay drug, not exclusively, especially out here in Kentucky, but still enough of a gay thing that it should be a giveaway as to what kind of tail the pastor was digging for.

And then of course they searched his computer and found the images and videos. Horrible stuff with underage guys, I even heard he had a snuff film, though that may have been just rumor. It didn't surprise me that the guy had all that shit. He seemed like the type to make this a regular practice, not to just do a one off kind of taking advantage of me kind of thing.

Once word did get out about where they found him and how, oh you best believe the kids at school had jokes. Ralph and Lloyd wouldn't stop calling him a faggot and laughing about it. Suddenly it went from a tragedy to a scandal, and scandals are funny in a way that tragedies are not. People ripped that guy a new one and didn't think twice about it, and the worst part was they called him a fag. They think that being gay and being a pedo are the same thing and they aren't. One is a natural way to have sex and the other is an immoral violation.

I didn't join in, which really did not help with the gay rumors but oh well. I decided it was best to just keep my mouth shut and have no opinion.

Oh but that didn't work, because the cops showed up to interrogate my ass anyway. I don't think they thought I was a suspect but these two cops, one a guy and one a lady, showed up at my house and had me sit without my parents in the living room while I told them what I knew.

"We just want to know what kind of a mental state he was in," they asked.

"Happy, I guess? I didn't know him that well."

"Did he ever," the lady cop paused. My mother had brought cups of coffee and a thing of milk and sugar to the detectives. "Thanks." The lady cop wouldn't talk until my mother left the room. "Did he ever, I don't know, say anything inappropriate to you?"

The man cop got real tense. Sat on the edge of the couch.

I thought back to our dozens of conversations, our hundreds of text messages, the images I had sent him, the way he spoke to me, and the word inappropriate seemed so inadequate, so insanely weak that I laughed when I said, "Nah, he didn't say nothing like that."

"Well, we're just concerned." Said the lady cop. She sipped her coffee, well dosed with milk and sugar. "Did you hear anything from the other boys at the church?"

"Nope."

She nodded a lot, like that told her something. She put the coffee down. "Look, Ezekiel. We know there was something going on. It seems like something people would talk about. Are you sure there was nothing, no words exchanged that might indicate...something?"

"You mean did we know he was a pedophile?"

"Well, yes. Did anyone know he was a homosexual?"

There it was again. Making them out to be the same thing. It made me angry, so mad that I wanted to grab her face and put it through my mom's glass table, but I held myself together.

"We all thought he was straight, sorry. But listen," now it was my turn to lean forward. "If I think of anything, or I hear of anything, I will absolutely let you know. I want this murderer found."

That satisfied the cops well enough and they left me alone from then on out, not knowing they had their guy right there in front of them. Dumbasses. Oh well, I should be so lucky.

"Just one thing," the man cop asked as he stood up. "Where were you that night?"

"What night? Oh, the night of the…? I was at home playing Call of Duty. Sorry."

Ben was freaked when I told him that I was talked to by the cops. We were laying in his bed and he was actually crying again, but I managed to calm him down and assure him that all was fine, that there was nothing going on and that there was nothing for either of us to be afraid of. He sniffed and nodded and was like, okay, which was good, except that when I stood up and put my pants on he asked me, "You wouldn't cheat on me, right?"

And since I didn't consider my weird hobby to be cheating I said "Nah, no way baby."

II

Then I went and fucked it up, because I let Ben come over and hang out and meet my parents one afternoon. He was wearing his Walmart uniform cause he worked later that evening and while my mother didn't have a problem with him and his raggedy black jeans and shaggy boy hair cut, my father definitely did. Oh he didn't say anything, just turned down Fox News when Ben walked into the foyer, but I could tell from the way he stared that he didn't approve. Fucker.

I gave Ben a tour of the house, and suddenly it occurred to me how different it was from how he lived, in a two-bedroom bungalow on a street with boarded up places. We had five bedrooms and three bathrooms and my dad had his own study and he was lining me up to inherit one of the BMWs when I got my learner's permit the next year. Our lives were nothing alike.

"Sorry," I said when I showed him my room. I had my own television and a desk with a gaming computer and everything.

"Why?" he responded in a way that let me know he understood what I meant.

"I don't know, never mind."

"You have a nice home," he said.

I grunted in the affirmative and sat down on the bed and kicked on my sound system. The bridge from one of Ben's tracks boomed out and his face lit up.

"You listen to my music?"

"Yeah? Why wouldn't I? It's good."

He sat next to me and put his head on my shoulder. I felt a sudden charge of fear so I got up and closed my door.

12

The one thing I'm ashamed of is that I tried to kill a woman one time. She legitimately didn't know I was underage. I met her on Tinder while she was swinging through town for this business trip, and so I met her at a restaurant. She was older, in her early thirties, and I'd never been with a woman before. I honestly can't tell if she was hot or not, like I think she was objectively attractive but I am just not into chicks. She made a comment about how I seemed pretty young, but I laughed it off. She'd already had a couple margaritas and when the waiter came by I ordered one too and the idiot brought one without checking my ID.

My plan was simple: Get her drunk, knock her out in the parking lot, drive her car out to the woods, tie her up, torture her, film it, then kill her. But something happened. We started talking and she told me about her ex husband and her young kids she didn't have custody of and how rough her life was, and I just started feeling bad for her. Like she didn't ask to have a rough life, and she hadn't done anything for me to kill her over.

The only reason I even thought about killing her is because I figured that's what most male serial killers did, they killed women, and so maybe if I was a serial killer I should kill a woman too. But what the fuck did she ever do to deserve a slow, painful death for? It didn't make sense to me. That's how I figured out I'm a revenge killer, a vigilante, not a serial murderer.

She tried to fuck me in the parking lot, in her rented Honda Accord. But I couldn't get it up, no matter how hard we both tried, and finally she just straight up asked me if I was gay.

"Yes," I said, and she was the first person I ever told.

"It's kind of shitty for you to go looking for women, then." she said.

"I'm sorry," I said. "I wasn't sure."

13

Things became more peaceful after I killed the pastor. I deleted the apps and stopped looking for targets. I figured I had done, perhaps, what I was put on this earth to do. I admit I did think of killing myself, but I didn't want to hurt my mom or Ben in the process. I figured that would be an evil thing to do and I didn't like to think of myself as evil, at least not back then.

The longer I saw Ben the harder it seemed for me to not come out as gay. He really wanted me to, after all he was open. We would argue about it for hours.

You're ashamed of me, he texted me one time. You don't want anyone to know that we're in love.

These kinds of texts irritate me. I don't like people being insecure around me, it's annoying. Why can't people just take me at my word? I'm not that dishonest. I texted him back and told him what I was thinking, that I just didn't feel safe outing myself at this point and that he would have to wait and see what happened next.

This wasn't enough to please him so I had to try really hard to calm him down and I promised him I would come over and help him feed his snake and all that, and it was kind of a pain in the ass except I guess maybe it wasn't, maybe I shouldn't talk about him like that.

But anyway yeah, things quieted down once people forgot about the scandal of the gay pastor. Life went back to normal and while I was a little bit worried about the cops I mostly figured they'd been snooping around just to get a feel for how dirty the old man was. So long as I played it cool there was no way that they would have come after me. Besides, I'd done such a good job of cleaning up, it was impossible for them to figure out who it was.

I thought about telling the shrink what I'd done, just to see if she'd write it off as a delusion one more time, but I figured that was probably pushing my luck just a bit too far. After all, she'd have to report it if there was anything authentic sounding to my confession, and I didn't need her going to the cops. Still, it might have been worth it to see the look on her face, if she actually bought it.

14

The way I'd fucked things up was that my dad told me he didn't want me to see Ben anymore. At first he didn't want to say why, just called me downstairs one time after getting home from work late and before he could even turn on Fox News he was just like, "I don't want you hanging around that Ben kid."

And I had to ask, "Why?" cause there was no way I was just letting it go.

"He's from a different background. I don't want you hanging around people that will bring you down."

Of course I asked what he meant, and he didn't want to say. I wanted to hear him say that he was poor, or gay, or something like that, but he just wouldn't say and finally he blew up at me and was just like, "Because I said so." And that was it, suddenly I was banned from seeing my boyfriend, and you know this pissed me off.

So I texted Ben and told him and of course he freaked out on me again, called me and started crying, and I had to console him and tell him that there was no way I was going to let my dad get in between us, that I would just lie about where I had been and they would have to deal with it, that we would definitely find a way to be together and that was that.

And that's how I thought it was going to be. I really meant it when I said I would find a way for us to be together, but then I realized that it wasn't really possible for things to go that way. I got really paranoid, see, I just got really paranoid that my dad was going to find out, so I started seeing Ben less and less. Of course that got Ben thinking I didn't love him anymore, which wasn't true, I totally did, but he didn't see it that way so he started smoking weed with his dad which really pissed me off. I mean, here he was, slagging off his old man for not caring about him, but now he was smoking weed with the guy. He'd start showing up to hang out stoned and I really wasn't feeling it, like it really bothered me. I wasn't sure what I was going to do about it but I wanted to do something.

Yeah, things weren't going so well between us at that point. And then the cops came back, and that scared me because they wanted to search my room, which instantly made my dad suspicious but of course they didn't find anything cause I'd thrown everything away, my bloody clothes, my knife, even the decent pair of AF1s I'd worn to do the deed.

So I was pretty stressed out and that's how I made the mistake of breaking up with Ben. He cried himself stupid over it, but I told him there was no way I could see him anymore, and anyway we'd only been seeing each other for like a couple months at that point anyway, but yeah I just couldn't handle the stress, and between that and the weed smoking he was doing I just wasn't feeling it anymore. Looking back now it was a dumbass decision on my part but I was going through a lot and didn't know what else to do.

15

I was actually really heartbroken after that. I got back on the apps, I don't know why, I think just because I felt so damn alone now that I wasn't going to Ben's place almost every day after school. I started working out a lot and like people started to take notice over the next couple months, I shaved my head, I kinda got weird to be honest. I got messaged by a lot of guys on the apps, I guess I had the body type they wanted now that I was working out, and while a lot of them were older there was this one guy who was 18 that I thought was kind of cute, some kind of metalhead guy that sort of reminded me of Ben, and I was like, yeah sure why not.

I really thought about killing him, except he didn't really seem to know how old I was and I didn't want to tell him. He said his name was Spike, which isn't a name but whatever, and I went over to his house after school one day and he lived in this real trash pit with another dude, just this absolute waste of a house, dirty dishes everywhere, empty soda cans, lots of weed smoke, and he offered me a beer and I didn't want him to think I was underage so I said sure and drank half of it, which was really gross.

I tried to talk to him about music but he didn't want to talk, which really bothered me. He was the kind of guy that collected vinyl, like all of it metal bands, and I recognized a couple names like Slayer and Iron Maiden and this one band Ministry that Ben was really into, and I would have liked to have listened to Spike's records and talked to him about music and stuff but he didn't care, he just wanted us to fuck.

So we did and it was kind of nice but we didn't cuddle after, didn't even talk, he just said he had to get to band practice right afterwards and didn't even invite me, so I said okay and went home and I gotta be honest, I cried a bit after that, which made me feel like a bitch, but I guess it's okay for men to cry too.

I deleted the apps after Spike cause I just couldn't handle it. I think I'm what the blue hairs on the internet call demisexual, like I only want to fuck people I'm into, except I'm gay and aren't gay men supposed to fuck a lot of different people? I don't know. Sometimes things are just weird and you have to accept that.

16

I told my mom I was gay not long after the thing with Spike. She made me go to the grocery store with her cause sometimes she's real fragile and can't like lift the cases of water and stuff, and I just blurted it out, the two of us sitting in her BMW SUV. I was just like "Mom, I gotta tell you something. I think I'm gay."
And she got real quiet for a bit, then she turned the car on and said "I kind of figured you were," in her weird French accent.

"You're not mad?"

"What difference does it make if I'm mad or not? You'd still be gay."

Well there was no arguing about that, so we drove home in absolute silence, no radio or nothing, but right when we pulled into the garage she said "Don't tell your father."

"Does he know?"

She got real quiet again. "Don't tell your father."

17

The cops came by yet again and this time they gave me the third degree. They wanted to know not just where I was the day of the murder but also where I'd been the weeks before, the weeks after, like how often I'd seen the pastor, what kinds of things we talked about when I did see him, all of it. Really it was nuts, and I just sat there and kind of sweated it out. I'm starting to think they suspect me, which maybe isn't as far-fetched as I thought it was, because maybe I didn't do such a good job cleaning up and maybe I didn't get rid of my clothes and shit all that well.

Ben was avoiding me at school, which was really awkward, and Ralph noticed and started giving me shit that I'd broken up with my boyfriend, which was like super fucked up of him even though it was true, so I shoved him against a locker and when I went to punch he went like "Oh no, you're gonna make out with me, please don't, I'm not gay, don't get your AIDS on me!" And I kind of left him alone after that cause I wasn't even sure what to say to any of that, like what do you say to that kind of shit?

I missed Ben because he and I could have had a laugh about that kind of thing. He always laughs at the dumbest shit, like things that are super fucked up or weird, and I guess I'm kind of the same way, but it's harder to laugh about that kind of stuff when you're alone. So I just didn't laugh about it, it just made me feel shitty and I had to move on all on my own.

I tried to talk to him in between classes but he straight up ignored me. He's started wearing hoodies all the time and it makes me worry he's cutting again. He posted a song on Sound-Cloud that was fucking beautiful but was also clearly about us and it made me feel kind of violated and ashamed but also really sad, and I jerked myself off while listening to it, which was a strange thing to do but felt right in the moment.

It's possible that I was kind of depressed after everything that had happened. I didn't feel guilt or anything about the murders I've committed but I did feel guilty about breaking up with Ben. I mean, what did he do to deserve that, right? All he did was love the wrong person, and you can't control who you love. It wasn't fair for me to go after him like that, I can see that now, but I was horny and I liked him and I hadn't messed around with a guy in a while so like, what harm could it have possibly done? Well, a lot, I guess.

18

I've been liking boys since I was four and said I wanted to marry Batman. And then when I was seven I said my next door neighbor was my boyfriend. When I said that my dad got real quiet and was like no, he isn't, and tried to explain the difference between a boyfriend and a regular friend. But I still didn't get the message, I just went on liking boys, and when I hit puberty I waited to start liking titties and I never did, I just kept staring at the other guys' asses and lips, and it was like super fucked up and I cried and cried cause I didn't want to be gay, in fact I still cry about it sometimes, but no matter what I do it won't go away, I just don't like girls.

Oh you know what's really the worst, is Ben kind of likes girls! Yeah he said he made out with one once and really, really liked it, back at his old school, and I just couldn't believe that but that's what he told me. I get jealous sometimes when he says a girl is hot but not when he lusts after like Trent Reznor or someone like that, the guy from Nine Inch Nails. It's weird but I kind of just accept it.

19

The cops showed up at school and let me tell you, I ran. I ran, and I stole a kid's bike, and I got the fuck away from school.

How it happened was I saw the two detectives, the lady cop and the man cop, waiting outside my science class, and I immediately knew why they were there and I booked it the fuck out of there. I don't know whose bike I stole but I didn't care, I just needed to get as far away from that place as possible. I rode it all the way to the other side of town to Ben's house. He had not shown up to school for like three days so I knew he was probably at home. I got off the bike and pounded on the door until he answered, wearing Cookie Monster pajama pants and a black shirt that said "Skinny Puppy" on it.

"I need your help," I said and I just let myself into the house.

"Why are you here?"

"Just please let's go and I'll tell you."

He didn't say anything, just followed me to his room. There was a joint lit by his computer and he was making a track. The snake banged himself against the glass of the tank, and I could smell cum underneath the powerful odor of weed smoke. Ben sat down at his computer and kept working.

"I need you to help me get out of town. The cops are after me."

He turned to me, acting like he didn't care but clearly freaked out. "Oh fuck."

"Yeah, and we need to go like now."

Ben didn't say anything, just kept working on his track. Finally he closed the laptop. "This isn't a joke, right? Like you showing up after dumping me and then asking for my help to run away, this isn't a joke?"

"No." I said. "This is real."

He nodded. "Okay. Just let me feed my snake."

Ben packed a bag while the snake gnawed and swallowed the rat. I kind of bounced up and down, willing him to move faster. He moved way slower than he used to, now that he was smoking weed all the time. I helped him pack the laptop so we could get out of there faster.

We got into his pickup truck and drove north on 41, not stopping until we crossed the Ohio River into Indiana, where we got energy drinks and gas. He wanted to find a motel there but I made him keep driving so we didn't stop again until we got to some tiny town outside of Indianapolis.

We slept in a Walmart parking lot, leant against each other. Before I drifted off I heard him ask me where we were going.

"I just need you to get me to Canada," I said. "I'll figure it out after I get there."

"That's a dumb fucking idea."

"Okay. Maybe I don't have a plan."

We were quiet in the LED gloom, the same lights that had belted down at us at Ben's old job.

"Does this mean we're back together?" Ben asked.

"Yeah," I said.

20

W e just kept driving around the next couple days. My mom kept calling me but I wouldn't answer my phone, in fact I'd turned it off so I wouldn't be able to be tracked. We lived off of shit we bought or stole from the various Walmarts and gas stations we ran into as we drove around the Midwest. We weren't exactly sure where we were going but we knew that there was no way we could go back.

I didn't want to tell Ben about why the cops were after me and he didn't ask but finally, after like a full two days of driving I decided to tell him. So I broke down the whole thing to him, about how I'd sort of lured in the pastor and then cut him up. Ben got real quiet and then finally said, "So you did cheat on me."

We were at a rest stop in Illinois. We were on our way to Chicago because Ben really wanted to see it again since that's where he'd been living before his mom died.

"I didn't cheat on you. I didn't fuck him."

"Yeah but you sent him pictures and stuff."

"Okay but I didn't...did you hear what I just told you? I killed the pastor. And I liked it."

Ben went silent again and drank from his Rockstar. "Are you going to kill me?"

I reached across the metal table and grabbed his wrist. "Fuck no, dude. I love you, okay?"

And I really meant it. I'd never loved anyone before but I was definitely in love with him. So he smiled and we cleaned up the potato chip bags off the table and got back in the truck.

We made it to Chicago. He wanted to go to the Museum of Contemporary Art so we found parking and went in there. There was this exhibition by a sculptor that Ben had heard of that did really gnarly shit with metal and so we went and took a look at it, Ben explaining to me what each of the pieces meant, and I wasn't sure that I totally bought his explanations but I was like cool. I like that he's into art and all that stuff, it's really nice, even if I don't get his art and he doesn't get mine.

"This one is about how like, sex and death are the same thing."

I looked at it. It was the biggest piece there, this like giant twisting mass of cut scrap metal, two shapes intertwined but not touching each other at all, just kind of going in and out of each other.

"Cool."

We stopped for hot dogs and ate them in the pickup and "Possum Kingdom" came up on my Spotify and I made him turn it up. He likes that song as much as I do.

"It's about a guy killing a girl," he said.

"No it's not," I said. "It's about a vampire."

That led to a fifteen minute argument that eventually got us laughing at each other, covered in mustard, and it was a nice moment where we didn't have to think about anything that was going on, anything that could have been bothering us, the real reason we were so far from home.

I still didn't want to stay in the city so we drove up to Wisconsin and found a tiny town and a motel to stay at. We had been sleeping at rest stops but both of our necks really hurt and we just really wanted to sleep in a bed. So we got a motel room and we took a shower together, which was really nice, and then he went and dried his hair which I didn't have to do on account of my shaved head. I turned the TV on to the news and they were talking about the pastor.

My heart started pounding but I controlled my breathing and watched the news report. They found the guy, they said. The guy that killed the pastor. I recognized the photo. It was Spike, the one from the apps that I hooked up with, and there was no talk about me whatsoever.

I yelled for Ben who cut the hair dryer and came pounding out of the bathroom. "What happened?"

I pointed at the TV. He sat down next to me, lower half wrapped in the other towel.

"So you didn't kill him?"

"No, I totally did. They just pinned it on the wrong guy."

Ben turned and looked at me. "Zeke. Are you sure you killed this guy? Like, are you sure you did it and you just didn't need an excuse to run away?"

"No way. I definitely killed him."

"You don't have to pretend. You can tell me the truth."

"I wouldn't lie to you, I swear."

But I wasn't as certain as I made it out to be. I wasn't positive that I wasn't delusional, that I hadn't made up the whole thing in the aftermath of finding out the guy had been murdered. Suddenly I was doubting my whole thing, everything I believed in, and I'd wished I'd listened better to my shrink but it was too late now. I don't know, but it had seemed real at the time.

"Well, it doesn't matter," said Ben. "We can go home now."

He got up and started to get dressed.

"No," I said. "I don't think I want to."

Ben turned and looked at me, half clothed. He stared at me, and didn't say anything, and he didn't have to say anything because it was clear what was going on. And he nodded, and we understood each other.

21

We headed up to Milwaulkee after that, why I don't know. I guess we just needed a place to go. I hated Milwaulkee when I lived there, not that I like Kentucky any more. Both of them suck in different ways.

I was kind of annoyed that Ben didn't believe me when I said I was a killer, and so I kept thinking of ways I could prove it to him. It just bothered me that he thought I was a liar or crazy or something like that, when really I was totally sane. Eventually a plan started to come together, of a way that I could show that I wasn't insane and that I was capable of murder.

We drove around all day and I showed him my old school and some places I had some sentimental feeling towards. I showed him my favorite place to get ice cream and so we stopped and got some as a treat. I got mint chip in a waffle cone and he got two scoops of coffee with chocolate shell and we sat in the truck and ate and I had some on my nose so he licked it off.

I turned my phone back on and it blew up with missed calls and texts that I ignored. I re-downloaded Grindr and I made a profile and before long I had a bunch of messages and more dick pics than I ever wanted to see. I messaged some of them back, mostly at random, though I definitely went for the oldest guys first. But what I did differently this time is that I outed myself. I told them how old I was, which I knew put me at risk of getting banned, but before long I found a guy.

I'm 14.

I don't care

He gave me an address and a time to meet him at and right after that I got banned from the app, which was fine because I had gotten what I needed.

Ben and I went to an under-21 nightclub and because it was like the middle of the week they let us in without even checking to see if we were 18 or not. We danced a little which was nice, Ben is a surprisingly good dancer even if I'm not. There was definitely at least one guy there checking us out which of course bothered me, I hate being ogled no matter the context.

Ben went to the bathroom and left me sitting at a table near the bar, but he was gone a really long time so I went to check and see if he was smoking. I found him outside on the patio in a corner with the guy who was checking us out, sharing a joint.

"What the fuck?" I said.

Ben's eyes got really wide and he quickly handed it back to the guy. I pushed the guy on the shoulder who didn't do anything, just kind of looked at me in stoned wonderment. He was a really faggy type too, and kind of creepy even though he was young, like who goes to a nightclub alone during the week?

Ben got between us cause he was obviously afraid I was gonna start a fight but the guy just shrugged and walked off, didn't say nothing. He clearly didn't want to get involved in whatever was going on between us.

"What was that?" I asked Ben.

"I can smoke if I want," he said to me, half mumbled cause he was stoned.

"Yeah, but with that creep?"

Ben turned away from me and looked like he was going to cry, but instead he just said, "Ok," and he let me hug him and the whole thing kind of blew over.

He said he wanted to sleep in a bed again so we should go to a motel, and I said that was fine, but I was worried about money. He told me not to worry about it, which was fine. I checked my phone and I could see it was almost time.

"Hey," I said, "Let's go. I'll show you where I grew up and we can get a motel room."

"Fine."

We went back to his truck. I gave him the address and as he drove I opened his glove compartment and rooted around in it.

"What are you looking for in there?"

I found a pocketknife and slipped it into my jeans. "Nothing. Just curious."

The neighborhood started to get sketchy and I would have been worried except I was so hyped up on adrenaline my ears were pounding. Ben got quiet and I could tell he was starting to get scared. The houses we passed by were mostly boarded up and there was almost no one on the streets. There weren't many streetlights so it was super dark.

"Here," I said. Ben pulled the truck over and we looked out the window.

"You grew up here?"

The address the guy had given me was for a house that wasn't boarded up but was clearly abandoned, which I thought was super weird and I hadn't been planning on.

"It was nicer back then." I got out of the truck. "You coming or going?"

He got out too and together we walked up the porch and to the front door, which was hanging open. We let ourselves inside. There wasn't much in the way of furniture of course, and there were holes in the floor and rats crawling around everywhere, it was gross. Suddenly there came a voice, calling out to us.

In the living room there was a man, the 45 year old man I'd picked up on the app, his lower half completely naked, on all fours, his hairy asshole in the air staring at me. His sad wrinkled balls hung below and I smelled something pungent that I suddenly realized was him.

"Zeke, what the shit?"

"It's okay."

The guy grunted. "Oh, you brought a friend. That's cool. Just hurry up and fuck me."

Ben said nothing, just stared at me in fear and loathing. I smiled and pulled the pocketknife out of my jeans.

"No." Ben reached out and grabbed my hand. I pulled and pushed and tried to shake him off but he was surprisingly strong. But I was stronger. I threw him off and sent him sprawling. I turned to the guy's asshole and stabbed the knife into it.

I can't really describe the sound the guy made, but I still think about it sometimes. He twisted, yanking the knife out of my hand, and jumped up with it still between his cheeks. He reached around to pull it out and honestly it was so funny, watching the guy trying to yank a knife out of his hole, that I started laughing. Which pissed him off and he made a move as if to chase me but I was faster and I grabbed Ben and pulled him to his feet and we dived into the truck as the guy hobbled after us, half naked with a knife still sticking out of his ass, onto the lawn and as Ben drove away, cursing me out to the ends of the Earth, I laughed and laughed until I cried.

22

Ben, he kind of went back and forth over whether or not he was going to talk to me in the next 24 hours. At first he tried to break up with me but I talked him down from that. We did stay at a motel after all and while he didn't want to mess around and got a room with two beds so he didn't have to sleep with me, he still didn't make me leave or anything so I figured we would be okay.

I felt a little sorry and told him so. I told him that I just wanted to prove that I was who and what I said I was but he just shook his head and told me no, that I wasn't anything like that. That I was just a sick fuck trying to play at being a serial killer. Which really annoyed me but whatever, I figured he'd calm down and we'd be fine.

We took off headed west. I don't know where we were going. But about an hour outside of Milwaukee, Ben pulled over on the side of the highway and parked the car.

"What? I said.

"You need to call your mother. If you don't, I'm taking you right back to Kentucky."

So I did, just to keep him happy. She wanted to know where I was and I wouldn't tell her, I wouldn't tell her who I was with or why I had left, I just wanted her to know I was okay.

"Put dad on the phone," I told her.

She said okay, and handed the phone over to my father. "You had better come back at once," he said. "I don't care where you went or who you went with, I just want you to come home right now."

"I'm gay," I told him.

He paused. "I don't care. Does it sound like I care? Look, all I want is for you to come home. I know you think you're grown but you're 14 years old. Please come back."

Whatever I expected from him, it wasn't that. I thought the would disown me, kick me out, tell me to go fuck myself, anything but wanting me back. I told him I'd think about it and I hung up the phone and got back in the truck.

"You know," said Ben, "My father hasn't called me once, since we've been gone."

And all of a sudden it clicked for me, how lucky I was, how blessed, how my family wasn't really that bad at all and I was actually kind of privileged, and suddenly I felt like a huge piece of shit and I couldn't help it and I started crying.

Ben stared at me.

"What?" I said.

"It's just weird, seeing you cry."

I punched him on the arm, not hard, really playfully, and he laughed, and then I laughed, and he pointed the truck towards home without me having to tell him which way to go.

23

I don't want to be like, happily ever after, here. I still killed a guy and let them stick it on some other dude. I broke up with my boyfriend and even though we got back together I still don't think he trusts me, even though my dad is fine with him now, mostly. Ben's dad straight up did not know he was gone. It's the weirdest shit, but Ben wasn't surprised by it at all, like it was exactly what he expected from his dad. I guess that's kind of just how it is, with them.

Ben's SoundCloud is lowkey blowing up. He's started playing shows around towns down here. It's pretty cool, actually. He gets hit on a lot, which is kind of surprising, like who knew industrial producers have groupies? But I'm not jealous. I know we belong together, that's just how it is.

The cops, it turned out, just wanted to notify me that they'd caught the killer. Apparently they're convinced he molested me. I don't see any reason to disabuse them of that notion.

The worst part about all of this is that I decided I should come clean to somebody, and so I told my shrink about what happened, that I was totally convinced I had killed the pastor and had stabbed that other guy in the asshole. And she told my parents, and they kind of put me in the hospital. I'm still there right now, which is why I'm writing all this, like I got a lot of free time.

It was a whole process. They dragged me to court and everything and the judge ruled that I needed help. They say that I'm delusional and they're worried in my confusion I might hurt myself, but that's bullshit. I think they're just scared of me, because secretly they believe that maybe I am a killer even if they won't admit it to me.

I don't know. This is what happened, and if they ever decide that I'm not lying and that I did kill those guys, I want everyone to know how it went down. I'm not ashamed of who or what I am. I'm a fag, and a killer, and ain't nobody gonna fuck with me and get away with it. *Nemo me impune lacessit,* and that's the truth.

A̲ ̲C̲ ̲K̲ ̲N̲ ̲O̲ ̲W̲ ̲L̲ ̲E̲ ̲D̲ ̲G̲ ̲M̲ ̲E̲ ̲N̲ ̲T̲ ̲S̲

The following stories were previously published elsewhere, sometimes in altered forms.

WOUND in Exposition Review

SANGUINISTA in five:2:one

LOVELESS in Flapperhouse

MANIA SEASON in Black Telephone Magazine

SHAGGING FLIES IN BALLARD in X-R-A-Y

Alexandrine Ogundimu

is a Nigerian-American transgender writer from Indiana.

She lives in the zeitgeist.

PUBLISHED BY FERAL DOVE BOOKS

ISBN 979-8-9856764-3-3

Thank you for being here.
Cover & Book design by Evan Femino

feraldove.com